DEADLINE

AKA DEADLINE FOR A DREAM

THANE & MOSS MYSTERIES
BOOK 1

BILL KNOX

ZERTEX
CRIME

DEADLINE

ISBN: 978-1-912767-79-3

Published worldwide by Zertex Media Ltd.
First published as DEADLINE FOR A DREAM in 1957.
This edition published in 2024.

1

FOREWORD

I first encountered Bill Knox in a second-hand bookshop in Inverness, twenty-odd years after his death.

I was browsing the shelves while hiding from the inevitable Autumn Highland rain, idly looking for nothing in particular. Randomly, I pulled out a battered old hardback and read the title: 'Death Department.'

Intrigued, I flicked through a few pages, discovering that it was part of a series of 1950s Glasgow-set police procedural novels. I read a few pages, then a few more.

Somewhere between pages one and fifty, the rain must have stopped.

I bought the book, brought it home with me to Fort William, and forgot all about it while I worked on the next book in my own DCI Logan crime fiction series. I then 'rediscovered' the book while doing my traditional post-writing office tidy, where I clear away the weeks of clutter that have accumulated while I've been hammering away at the keyboard.

I'd spent almost a full ten minutes tidying by that point, so I felt I had earned a break. After clicking on the kettle to make a cup of tea, I sat down, skimmed the pages I'd read in the shop, then carried on with the story.

A few hours later, I'd finished the book. I hadn't even bothered to get up and make the tea. Which, as my wife will attest, is practically unheard of.

I had been expertly drawn into the world that Bill had created, and was right there alongside detectives Thane and Moss as they carried out their investigations. I had identified with the detectives right away – the imposing Chief Inspector Colin Thane, with his no-nonsense attitude and dogged determination, and his trusty Inspector, Phil Moss, whose loyalty to his friend was second only to his worries about his grumbling ulcer.

They immediately felt like real people. More than that, they felt like real Scottish men, whose evident care for one another was masked beneath gruff exchanges and barbed banter.

Despite the books being written over half a century before, these were the people I was writing about. Bill's Thane and Moss could have been my own DCI Logan and DI Ben Forde.

Yes, some of the terminology was different, and there was a lot less swearing in Bill's book, but down below the surface, down where it mattered, we were both writing about good but complicated men doing their best to bring killers to justice.

More than that, we were writing about the relationships between those men, and how their experiences affected them and those around them. We were writing gritty, gripping stories, but with a seam of very dark, very Scottish humour running through them.

I went online to order some more in the series, and to my dismay found that they were very difficult to get hold of. I managed to hunt some down from second-hand booksellers, off eBay, and from Amazon resellers, but they were often in poor condition, sometimes with pages missing – and, in one instance, with four chapters of an entirely different book by another author inserted upside-down at the back.

So, I turned detective myself. Digging around, I discovered that the books were all out of print. At that point, I had quite recently established my own publishing company, solely dedicated to publishing my own books.

'But what if I didn't just publish my own books?' I thought. What if I could use my publishing company to bring Bill's books back into print for modern audiences?

Bill passed away in 1999, and I was unable to track down details of his agent. Emails and calls to his old publishers went unanswered. Several months passed, and I was just beginning to fear that I'd reached a dead end when I managed to get the contact details for Bill's daughter, Susan.

Susan, thankfully, was delighted by the idea of us bringing her late father's work back into print, and it was while chatting to her that I realised the similarities between Bill and me extended beyond our crime novels.

We were, and are, arguably too prolific for our own good! Bill wrote countless novels under several pen names. I've written over two hundred books using dozens of pseudonyms. Like Bill, I've often switched between genres. Like Bill, I've had a blast doing all of it.

One of Bill's pen names was even Michael Kirk! Maybe he's some sort of literary relation...

Bill found early success when he became the youngest-ever Glasgow journalist at the age of just 16. At the age of 17, I sold my first piece of written work – a monster movie screenplay set in the Highlands of Scotland called Curse of the Bog Women.

We were and are both family men, with a shared love of Golden Retrievers.

There is some debate over whether he invented it, but Bill

is widely accepted as having been the one to bring the word 'neds' to the public consciousness. One of my characters, Bob Hoon, is also responsible for some interesting additions to the English language, but none that I can repeat here.

We are both multi-talented – as well as being a journalist and author, Bill went on to become the face of STV's Crimedesk and Tales of Crime shows. Along with writing, I'm quite good at putting things on and removing things from high shelves.

The similarities are truly uncanny!

I am very proud to be able to bring you the reissued Thane & Moss novels, starting with Deadline, which was originally published as Deadline for a Dream in the UK, and In For the Kill in the US.

Bill's family believes he'd be delighted that his books are being published all over again, and we're all excited at the thought of Colin Thane and Phil Moss being introduced to a whole new audience of readers.

Aside from the slight change to the title, and a few ten-thousand-word chapters being broken into shorter segments, the book you are about to read is the same one first published in 1957.

So, stick the kettle on, get the biscuits out, and settle down to enjoy not just a fantastic detective novel, but a genuine slice of Tartan Noir history from one of Scotland's true master storytellers.

Best wishes,

JD Kirk

CHAPTER ONE

THE YOUNG POLICEMAN was rising out of the car seat, fumbling for his baton with a desperate, automatic courage, when the stranger shot—shot to kill.

The report, sharp, crisp, drowned the youngster's half-formed words, ending them in a grunt of exploding pain.

While it still rang in the ears of the other two men in the car, the uniformed body, jerking, then suddenly limp, half-fell the rest of the way out of the Rolls Royce's opened door. It thudded to rest, one leg unnaturally twisted and balanced between car and pavement.

The dark blue police cap, with its blue and white diced band, rolled in a wild half-circle on the ground. The baton clattered on the running-board.

The constable was twenty-three years of age, fresh-faced... and dead.

Dumbly, stiffly, urgently, the stranger moved forward.

Behind the mask, his face was twisted with emotion, beaded with the sweat of terror. He took three steps to the side of the car and waved the automatic again.

'Open that rear door. Quickly. That'—his head jerked towards the body at his feet—'was a fool. Don't make me shoot again.'

The cashier had seen death at close quarters many times, long years ago at Ypres, on the Somme. He knew that death once more waited at his elbow.

Jerking his fear-frozen left arm to life, he slipped back the locked door handle, swung open the rear door of the car, then involuntarily shrank away.

The stranger, a slim, medium-built man wearing a dirty raincoat and woollen gloves, eyes bright behind his grotesque mask, stretched into the car with his left hand, the right hand waving the automatic in a slow arc between the cashier and the bottle-green uniformed figure of the chauffeur seated in front.

He ignored the two bulky canvas bags lying on the rug-covered floor and scooped up the black leather bag lying beside the chauffeur's feet.

Once more the stranger waved the gun, and in his half-muffled, strained voice repeated the warning, 'I don't want to shoot. Stay where you are.'

He ran the few yards to where the motorcycle lay on its side, stuffing the gun into the pocket of his raincoat as he went. Left arm threaded through the wide handles of the bag, trapping them in the crook of his elbow. He had the bike upright and was pounding the kick-starter before the men in the car came out of their daze.

The bike sputtered to life at the third kick. The stranger twisted the throttle, the engine roared, and the machine, rider crouching low, shot past them, bounced over the pavement, and skidded into the lane from which it had come long seconds before.

The cashier gave a faint moan and began to scramble out of the open door. His driver, tumbling across the front seats, joined him, and for long moments they bent over the huddled figure lying beside the car. Gently, they turned the body over... and their eyes met in horror.

'He's—he's...' the cashier broke off, staring in awed disbelief at the blood staining his hands.

Two of the car's tyres were flat, punctured by bullets, and the lane was too narrow, anyway, to allow it to pursue.

The chauffeur, cursing, began to run after the raider, the cashier following. Yet, even as they reached the opening, only a few yards away, they knew their bid was useless.

Down the length of the lane came an echoing roar as, having gained the next street, the rider turned into its width. Engine bellowing under the strain of being held in torturing peak revs through every gear in a desperate desire for speed, the motorcycle screamed along the tarmac.

It was the driver who took command. He turned to the still-stunned cashier, shrugging his shoulders. 'The only thing we can do is to get to a phone and call the police and an ambulance... not that the ambulance will do any good. But I caught the bike's registration number. That'll help.'

Then, as another, more urgent, thought struck him, 'How much did the swine get, sir?'

'Seven thousand pounds,' half-whispered the white-faced cashier, his whole body beginning to shake as he groped for his cigarette packet in a blind reflex. 'But that devil with the clown mask... the money doesn't matter. That man's dead. Oh my God, he's dead.'

For long, agonising seconds they stared at each other in bewildered disbelief. Then, almost mechanically, they turned from the lane, back towards the car.

As the two men turned, a lorry, travelling down the street from the opposite direction, drew to a sudden halt beside the Rolls and its solitary, lifeless companion. A green and white mufflered haulier jumped from the cab and ran with clattering boots across the roadway.

The lorryman bent for a closer look, then hurriedly crossed himself.

Just over two minutes had passed, and apart from the lorry and its driver, the roadway was still deserted.

CHAPTER TWO

AT ALMOST THE same moment as the lorryman was dialling 999 from a small dairy shop, David Renfield, bag still over his arm, gun in pocket, was quietly steering the motorcycle off the road and onto a patch of waste ground a mile and a half distant.

On the horizon, vague through the smoke and haze, he could see the cranes and chimneys of Clydeside. Near at hand, an engine chuffed along a railway embankment, pulling a long string of goods wagons.

To one side of the patch of ground a tenement turned its blank, windowless chimney wall towards him. On the other, the high stone spire of a church soared skywards.

But on the ground itself, almost completely shielded from the road by a battery of advertising hoardings, a mongrel dog, sniffing round an old cardboard box, was the only living thing in sight.

Switching off the bike's engine as it drew alongside the silver-grey Ford shooting brake which he had parked there less than half an hour before, Renfield balanced the machine on its stand and laid the bag on the ground.

Taking the key from his pocket, he unlocked the wide back doors of the brake and threw them open. Then, summoning all his strength, he seized the bike by the handlebars, lifted the front end, and got the front wheel onto the platform of the vehicle. Grunting at the exertion, he pushed and heaved, and finally got the machine completely aboard.

Scrambling in beside it, he hurriedly draped a waiting canvas sheet over it, then, dropping to the ground again, carefully closed and locked the doors, and, picking up the stolen bag, went round to the driver's door, opened it, got in, and quickly started the engine.

It had been smooth and slick, as it had had to be, as he had planned and replanned it all these weeks... planned every detail of it, except for that uniformed body slumping from the Rolls.

But there was no time to think of that, thank God. Not yet.

With unsteady fingers he slipped the gear lever into first, and let the brake purr and sway gently over the weed-covered surface, across the pavement and into the road.

He had the engine in top gear and was travelling south at just under 30 m.p.h. when a black police patrol car, a Jaguar, flashed towards, then past him. The white-gauntleted driver and his companion, the latter busily talking into a microphone, spared not a glance for the car.

"I've done it, I've done it," he told himself. "Slowly, carefully now—mustn't bump into something or go through a halt sign. That's the crazy sort of thing that could wreck everything.

"If I could open that bag... but that's not on the plan. Not till I get back to the lock-up and get the car away."

And the plan, he knew, must be obeyed at all costs.

The plan.... It had first taken shape in Renfield's mind one morning over a month before when the 29-year-old reporter, on the staff of the Evening View, had been having a casual 10 a.m. cup of tea in the canteen at Glasgow police headquarters.

The big room, reserved for sergeants and constables, with pressmen having an unofficial membership right, was quiet. Sergeant Breaden, a bulky six-footer, joined him at the small plastic-topped table, in an affable mood. His good humour had been brought about by just seeing a pet "ned"—a descriptive phrase which covers the multitude of Glasgow's lesser louts—sentenced by the Sheriff to six months' imprisonment for assault.

The "ned" in question had attacked another gentleman whose worth to the community was of rather negative value.

The sergeant and a constable had hauled the attacker off his victim just before the traditional coup de grâce of a kick on the head from a heavy boot was about to be applied.

'How's it going, David?' asked the sergeant, who knew Renfield of old as "police calls" man for the View, responsible for the gathering of routine information from various police channels, collector of tit-bits in the form of safe-blowings and sudden deaths in quiet times, by-line crime reporter when big news reared its head in the city.

'So-so,' replied Renfield. 'The Lost Property Department have a couple of sheep on their hands—the four-legged variety. A character found them on his tenement landing this morning, practically swore off the booze before he found they were real. They'll have strayed from the Meat Market, I suppose.'

'Aye, things are always quiet in mid-week,' agreed the sergeant. 'Thursday onward till Sunday morning is our busy part of the week. Thursday's the day when the thugs are on the assault and robbery prowl, flat broke and knowing there are plenty of places sending out for Friday's wages, or banking their takings.

'Friday morning—that's the time when all the overnight safe-blowings are discovered. The "petermen" have a ruddy genius for smelling out firms with tin-can safes and a habit of drawing their pay packet money on Thursday.

'As for Saturday—anything can happen then, and usually does, especially after the pubs are shut. The backwash of all the drunken brawls don't die away till pretty near dawn on Sunday. But after that, at any rate, we get time to collect our thoughts.'

Renfield, agreeing with the sergeant's summing-up, commented, 'And the shocking thing is that none of our local crooks seem to have any respect for evening paper edition times. If it's a street robbery, they always do it about ten minutes before the last edition. If it is a safe-blowing, then they make so much noise that it is discovered almost immediately, and the morning papers get first nibble at the story. You should train them better than that, Sergeant.'

'What really riles me is the senseless way in which shop-keepers send these unguarded messengers to the banks,' growled the sergeant.

'We get the same thing happening every week,' he complained, pouring some more milk into his cup, and unwrapping the little parcel containing his mid-morning sandwich.

'These idiots send a kid of about sixteen along to the bank with a nice big bag of lolly to put away, or a packet of money to collect for wages. They send them out at the same time, over exactly the same route, and always the same wee girl—or, at the best, some old fellow the wrong side of sixty. Then the fools wonder when some bunch of spivs clatter their messenger over the head and get away with the loot.'

'Fair enough,' interrupted Renfield. 'But quite a few times you find that the sweet little girl or the dear old dad is in on the robbery and only got thumped over the head for effect.

'They get a lump on the skull—and a nice fat cut of the proceeds.'

'That does happen sometimes,' admitted the sergeant, then he looked up as another uniformed figure approached their table.

'Hello, here's old Lawson,' said Breaden, as the second sergeant joined them. 'Here, Jack, I was just telling the lad about the daft habits of our local shopkeepers when it comes to collecting money from the bank.'

Lawson sniffed, thumping down his cup and saucer on the table and pulling in a chair.

'Aye, and believe me, the big firms are just as bad,' he agreed. 'Take Swivneys.'

Renfield forced a look of intelligent anticipation on his face, though he had troubles enough without having the moans of the city's police unburdened on him. Still, there might be a feature piece in it for the View, and McRowder, the news editor, faced with a bare diary and consequently crotchety, would be grateful.

'Take Swivneys,' said Sergeant Lawson again, gulping a mouthful of tea. 'They send out a ruddy great black Rolls Royce each Thursday afternoon with a chauffeur and cashier, pick up their payroll—must be about seven thousand pounds, it's for the entire factory—then drive back again. They are out in the ruddy wilds of factoryland, yet they use the same back-streets route every week, the same car, and only one poor devil of a young cop to guard the lot. One day some of these London car bandits are going to come up here and knock off the whole payroll.

'You know what the streets are like in that part of Glasgow... only the odd lorry or car now and again, quiet as the grave most of the time. That car's a sitting duck.'

The talk turned to football seconds later, and the two sergeants began arguing about the merits of the current Glasgow Rangers forward line. But Renfield was no longer listening. A wild, crazy notion had sprung into the young reporter's mind.

He made no mention of the sergeants' complaints when, an hour later, he returned to the View office. Head in an unsteady whirl of confused, half-formed ideas, Renfield entered the lift, stabbed the second-floor button, and waited impatiently till the cage stopped at the editorial flat.

He walked past the bustling subs' desk and over to the reporters' room. Waving a perfunctory greeting to the few reporters in at that hour, either just back from assignments or killing time until their particular tasks came round, he pulled his typewriter from its locker.

'Let's get rid of this junk, then maybe I can think straight,' he muttered, slipping paper in the machine and opening his notebook.

Apart from the mystery of the two sheep, there were only two small stories that had been handed out by the Enquiry Department at the police station. One sought witnesses of an accident, the other was an attempt to identify a lost memory case in a city hospital. But all the time he worked he was repeating to himself the sergeant's words—"The same route, the same time, the same car, and only one poor devil of a cop to guard the lot. The car's a sitting duck."

It was, so far, only a slender, colourless thread. But it might yet weave a moneyed pattern which could clear away his torment, a torment he alone knew existed.

There was the money, seven thousand pounds, the policeman had said, waiting, begging to be taken.

And there was Jean Catta, dark-eyed, full-figured, heady. Jean, with her passionate regard for gaiety and clothes, perfumed elegance and the good things of life. Jean, who was a fashion model with a doctor father, and who openly declared her intention of marrying only a man who, in addition to attracting her, could adequately supply the luxuries of life.

Renfield had first met her when her employer's shop had been broken into by a couple of thieves whose taste ran more to the contents of the petty cash box than the exclusive dresses lining the walls. She had posed for a couple of pictures after the manager had decided that the publicity from the break-in would be an asset to the end-of-season sale due to begin the following week.

'Like a copy of the pictures?' he had asked her, as the photographer arranged the scene to show the maximum of her figure and the minimum of the damaged desk from which the money had been taken.

She had eagerly accepted the offer. Back at the View, Renfield had to argue with the photographer, who was also young, single and interested in the dark-haired girl. Renfield finally won on the toss of a coin, and wandered up to the shop that evening, armed with an envelope containing two glossy prints of the pictures.

Jean had emerged, expressed surprise at the encounter and at his remembering his promise, and, after a moment or two, had agreed that the photographs must be discussed over a drink.

'Just a few minutes,' she had warned. 'I'll need to get home after that.'

The "few minutes" had ended at nearly midnight, with a promise of further meetings.

That had been some months ago. Renfield held Jean, temporarily at any rate, with the supposed glamour of his job as a crime reporter, with his hire-purchased car, and the way he was draining his savings in an effort to provide the silk-lined luxury which was demanded by Jean.

But just a few evenings previous, there had been a temperamental storm, one of several of late, all over the fact that Renfield, unexpectedly working overtime on a story, had turned up tired, dusty, and an hour late for their date. Jean had had to cool her heels in the restaurant lounge—and no explanation would reduce her rage.

She was bitter without being savage, tremulous without bursting into tears.

'I'm not used to this sort of treatment,' she had warned him. 'And I don't intend becoming used to it either.'

A beautifully worked silver charm bracelet and a long, appealing letter went to her home the next day. Between them they mended the break—but the bracelet sliced another nine pounds from Renfield's thinning bank account.

And he at last faced up to the fact that money, big money, was the only language which would ever really sway the girl. She was like a drug to him—overpowering, heady. But despite all the perils she threatened, he knew he had to have her—needed her with a craving that at times terrified him.

"Was this the solution? The same route, the same time, the same car, and only one poor devil of a cop to guard the lot."

CHAPTER THREE

THE EVENING when the idea first began mulling around in his mind was one when he had plenty of time on his hands.

Jean had scrapped a date they had made—instead she was going to a dinner-dance given by one of her father's wealthier friends, the type of outing she adored.

The bunch of newspapermen he sometimes spent the evening with were all either broke or had previous engagements. Renfield glanced through the cinema programmes... nothing there.

'Might as well go home,' he decided.

"Home" was the little house he lodged in at Southwood, on the outskirts of Glasgow. Mrs Senior, the landlady, delighted in mothering her boarder, but she was sensible enough to leave David Renfield strictly to himself when he obviously didn't feel inclined to tolerate company.

He got to the house about six o'clock, picked half-heartedly with knife and fork at the meal Mrs Senior had ready for him, and quickly retired to his small bed-sitting room. With a sigh he threw himself on top of the bed, and, lying there, let his eyes roam round the room. The four walls had been home to him for several years now, ever since he had finished his National Service and come to Glasgow from his home at Dundee to work on the View. His mother and father had been dismayed—in over thirty years they had never left their hometown except on their annual fortnight's holiday. Renfield had been on the local paper before he went to the army, and somehow, they had never thought of him wanting to go further afield. But, as usual, he had had his own way with them. They wrote once a week, he replied once a fortnight... and they thought there was no one quite so fine as their son.

"That's probably part of the trouble," he admitted to himself. "At home, well, I always got what I wanted. Now..."

He pulled a cigarette from his packet, lit it, and flipped the match across the room into the fireplace.

It had been different, all right, in the Army and then on the View. David Renfield might find things his own way back home. But as far as the big cruel world was concerned, he had to take his chance like anyone else. And Renfield, often boiling with frustrated rage within, always found that, after determining to take a firm stand, he capitulated when the time came to make an actual protest. It was easier, somehow, to accept the decisions made for him by the hard-faced strangers.

Where did it all get him? There he was, on twenty pounds a week, assets one half-paid car and about a hundred pounds in savings. Five foot seven in height, with dark hair and hazel eyes, he had a wardrobe of sports clothes plus one "best" blue suit for special occasions. Apart from the car, his only real debt was a small account owing to the bookmaker near his office, the penalty for a misplaced faith in the View's racing tipsters.

But there was a difference now. Jean had decided on him. This time things were for once going to be the way David Renfield wanted them. Getting that money would be more than a test of his ingenuity. It would be firm notice to the world that he was tired of being just another cog. And it would bring him Jean just as surely as pulling her in on a golden chain.

Pensively stroking his upper lip, he started to consider the problem that confronted him.

Renfield had been "in" on too many robbery investigations as a pressman to imagine that the police were fools. He had sat reporting too many High Court trials, had seen too many allegedly penitent prisoners sentenced, to be under any illusion as to the penalty for being caught. Scotland might not have a Dartmoor, but neither Barlinnie nor Peterhead prisons were holiday homes.

It would be a gamble. But the money at stake was a powerful goad, and careful planning might successfully reduce the odds against success.

He sat till late that night in his little room, scribbling, doodling on scraps of paper, discarding one scheme after another. When so sleepy he could no longer think clearly, he finally burned all the papers and prepared for bed, he still had no fixed plans. "But there will be a way," he told himself. "And I'll find it."

The following evening, he had another date with Jean—and this time it wasn't cancelled. He was to meet her at her home—she stayed with her father and mother in a block of flats in Pollokshields, once one of the more exclusive districts in the city, but now slightly soiled around the edges by age and decay. Renfield was at the house at seven sharp, armed with tickets for the new musical show at the King's Theatre. It was, for him, one of the happiest evenings for some time. At last, he was committed to action, action which would make the dark-haired witch beside him his own.

After the show they went on to supper. Renfield felt relaxed, peaceful, as Jean smiled and laughed, talking about the musical—even if a corner of his mind was calculating how long it might be before her mood changed.

But even when it did change, he knew the fascination, hypnotic in quality, would remain. "I know her temper. I know she's out purely for what she can get, but I'm still crazy about her," he told himself with an inward curse at his own weakness. And he knew only too well that if he could get the money to command her constant attention, the way it came about or the reasons for her capitulation wouldn't matter a damn.

CHAPTER FOUR

THERE ARE ways in which a newspaper reporter can obtain information about most things. Ways which are as simple as lifting the telephone, as direct as asking a point-blank question of a "contact." But these ways were ruled out for David Renfield when the information he sought crossed from the crime story inquiry into the crime planning category.

Renfield went it alone. His first, major lucky break was that his day off was by long agreement always on a Thursday.

That Thursday afternoon he was along at the Swivney factory entrance, apparently gazing at the windows of a nearby block of shops.

After a short wait, he saw the Rolls Royce sweep out at exactly 2.15 p.m. There was a chauffeur at the wheel, a uniformed constable beside him. In the back sat the cashier, a mild-looking middle-aged man.

Making a few small purchases in the shops, taking his time over each, gave Renfield cover until the car returned about an hour later.

That was stage one. It took another seven days, seven days

when work had become a dull, inescapable routine, before stage two in Renfield's plan.

His car was parked along the road a little from the factory that Thursday afternoon. Once more, at exactly 2.15 p.m., the Rolls drew away from the factory gates, the three men aboard. As it passed, Renfield started up the Ford, and followed the limousine at a distance along its back-street route, turning off at a road junction halfway towards the city centre. He turned the Ford again, and, back on the route, parked outside a block of offices and waited.

The Rolls swept back a little over half an hour later.

It took the same route coming and going! "The same route, the same time, the same car," just as the sergeant had said.

One more week he waited. Then came stage three. This time he picked up the payroll car at the office block near the city, tailed it through the heavy traffic on its inward journey—nearly losing it once at a set of traffic lights—and drove past as the Rolls halted outside a bank in Hope Street, in the centre of Glasgow.

Minutes later, after a scurry to find a place to park his car, he stood across the road from the bank and watched as the cashier came out of the swing doors. The man strolled across the pavement towards the chauffeur-guarded Rolls, a black leather grip in his hand, the constable at his side. The cashier made a second trip, and this time returned with two canvas bags, which Renfield guessed contained coins.

For a man with a mind trained for the everyday purpose of reconstructing crime and analysing occurrences, the rest was, up to a point, an easy reversal of normal processes.

There was a desolate half-mile stretch of road on the payroll car's route, running through a factory area, a street which, like many others in similar parts of the city, was used only occasionally by-passing traffic. An almost deserted street, with few windows overlooking it at any point, it seemed ideal for his purpose.

Then, driving over its length once more, he noticed the lane, leading between two huge factory yards to the next, slightly busier roadway. Though wider and with perhaps a little more traffic, it was still a place in which the atmosphere was oddly out of place with the bustle and clamour he knew was in progress in the buildings all around.

The lane provided another piece in the building jigsaw of robbery. Perhaps he could leave his car parked at the other end of it, rob the Rolls, and sprint through.

Other sections slid into place. Renfield had a gun, a shiny automatic which he had acquired just after the war from a drunken fellow soldier one night in a village pub near to their camp. The young reporter had been on National Sendee at the time, a despatch rider with the Royal Corps of Signals; proud of his marksmanship on the range and in a way frustrated with the knowledge that the fighting was over and honour and glory had faded, leaving only a type of Boy Scout camp existence which was as irksome as the discipline seemed childish.

A gun of his own, as distinct from one "on loan" from the Army, held a glamour that was satisfying to his adolescent ego. He had willingly paid five pounds, the Regular's price, to secure possession of the automatic, a trophy "liberated" during the Normandy invasion.

The glamour had faded, but the gun, and the loaded clips of ammunition that had come with it, remained, buried in a locked suitcase at his lodgings.

"If I can only think of a simple way to stop that car," he puzzled. "I wouldn't have to shoot. A wave of the gun at the men in it should be enough. It isn't their own money they are guarding... why should they risk their lives?"

Even if he had to fire, if the policeman acted tough, a flesh wound would surely end all resistance.

But how to stop that car, and how to best make his getaway, remained Everest-like obstacles.

Their solution came to him exactly ten days before the Thursday on which he made his bid.

CHAPTER FIVE

THE AMERICAN BAR was quiet at that early hour of the evening. Jean, in one of her more truculent moods, but still breathtakingly beautiful in a grey silk dress which did all kinds of things to his imagination, twirled her glass between her hands, obviously ill-tempered. Then it started—she began laying down the law about his needing a new car, and her dislike of his existing transport.

'Why can't you have a sports car like Ronnie Sett?' she complained, not adding that Sett's father happened to have a very nice chain of tobacco shops, and that Daddy could be guaranteed to agree to most of Ronnie's requests.

'That old shooting brake of yours is hardly fit to be seen in. It is about as bad as one of those filthy motorcycles you are always talking about.

'Couldn't you get one of those lovely little Triumph T.R.2S?' she went on.

For once, Renfield suddenly stopped listening to what she was saying. That entire jigsaw in his mind had just gone jump-

jump-jump, like one of those funny little advertising "shorts" on the cinema screen.

A motorcycle! With it he could stop the car. He could load it into the back of the brake, park the Ford some distance away, go the rest of the way on the bike, carry out the robbery, escape up the lane again—it was too narrow for a car to pursue him through—load the machine back into the brake, and drive off. The complete change of transport would throw the police wildly off the scent.

He could wait in the lane until the car appeared. There was a much more than even chance that there wouldn't be another vehicle on the road. At the critical moment he'd ride it out of the lane, onto the road, pretend to fluster, skid, and "ditch" the motorcycle a few yards in front of the Rolls. To a former despatch rider, it would be simplicity itself to do it without damaging himself or the bike.

The car would stop, its occupants concerned at the "accident"... and the gun would take care of the rest. A bullet through two of the tyres to disable the Rolls and show the strength of his argument would be the final touch.

The beauty of the plan was that he could take a motorcycle whenever he wanted, without anyone knowing. He shared a Nissen hut lock-up garage with a young motorcyclist who only used his somewhat neglected machine at the week-ends. A 200 c.c. *Dot*, it was fast, fairly light to handle, and would be easy enough to load or unload from the car.

It had more than a few scratches and dents about it, testimony to its owner's carelessness. Any light scraping the machine suffered in the fake fall would either pass unnoticed, or could be dismissed as having been caused by some accident in the lock-up.

'I'll need fresh number plates,' he murmured. 'It would be a complete giveaway if the originals were spotted.'

'David, what were you saying?' asked Jean. 'I don't believe you've been listening to a word I've been telling you.'

'Oh yes, I have, dear,' he told her. 'I was just wondering what price my car might raise if I sold it.'

'You mean you will get a new one?' beamed the girl, in a typical change of mood.

'Maybe, maybe,' he replied. 'I'll certainly think about it. It's worth considering.'

He made the number plates at home the next night, carefully following a pencil sketch he had made at the lock-up, a sketch which showed the necessary dimensions needed for the substitute plates, even the position of the necessary bolt- holes. Two pieces of plywood, some black cellulose and a small tin of white paint were the materials he needed, all purchased that day.

The worst part was the painting of the numbers. He needed several attempts before he got them right.

Then, when he finished, the smell of cellulose and paint was so strong in his room that he had to spend the night with the windows wide open, shivering in the cold, so that the air might be clear for the morning, when Mrs Senior would be in to tidy up.

The last thing he did before going to work the next morning was to place the almost-dry pieces of wood, which now looked exactly like the genuine articles, into the case beside the gun. He carefully locked the case again when he had finished. Mrs Senior could be trusted implicitly, but not the slightest risk could be taken which might imperil his venture.

There was one last, but all-important point. He mustn't be identified. That solution, too, fell into his lap.

Johnny Fellowes, who was on the industrial reporting desk, proudly produced a grotesque false face on the Monday afternoon, and proclaimed, 'It's Hallowe'en on Friday, boys. Look what I got for the youngster.'

Gazing at the leering green mask, with its protruding teeth and broad, twisted nose, he added, 'Here, isn't it just the image of our beloved news editor?'

Half an hour later, Renfield was in a nearby department store. One of thousands of people making similar purchases at shops throughout the city, he selected an adult-sized Hallowe'en mask, made of clinging rubber. Flesh-coloured, and milder than most of the false faces on display, it had a bright red nose as its main feature.

'Three shillings,' said the bored girl assistant, stuffing his purchase into a small brown paper bag, Accepting the money, she promptly forgot all about the transaction. She had already sold nearly five hundred masks that day, and was only concerned with the fact that her new shoes were making her feet throb with pain.

And, on the Thursday, his plan worked. He left the Ford in the patch of waste ground, which, shielded as it was, seemed perfect for his purpose. He unloaded the motorcycle, and rode on it to the lane. There, sheltered in the shadow of the walls he waited undisturbed for ten minutes, smoking a cigarette.

Two lorries passed, then a small, battered private car. Finally, at three o'clock, dead on schedule, the payroll car came along the otherwise empty road travelling at a sedate pace.

With a thrill of excitement, he slid the Hallowe'en mask over his features and started the motorcycle's engine.

Renfield kept the machine ticking over in the lane until almost the last second. Then, with a bark of the throttle, he shot the *Dot* out of the shelter of the wall, across the pavement, bounced over the kerb, and turned onto the road, in the same direction as the car was heading.

The Roll's horn bellowed an alarmed protest. At the same

time Renfield threw the *Dot* into a wavering skid, then, almost lowering the bike to the ground, slid off in a roll which was as spectacular as it was harmless.

The brakes of the car had hardly stopped squealing, the opulent, distinctive radiator arrested only about ten feet from the bike's still spinning wheels, when Renfield, springing to his feet and jerking the gun from his coat pocket, fired twice. At each report a bullet hit one of the nearside tyres. They collapsed on the spot.

In the car, the policeman, concern on his face, had thrown open the door, ready to help the "injured" motorcyclist. The cashier had just exclaimed: 'The young fool...' The chauffeur, foot still hard on the brake pedal, was getting ready to say what he thought of motorcyclists in general.

At the shots, the policeman seemed to grow suddenly smaller, younger, as he saw the gun, still smoking and now pointed towards him, and realised what was happening.

'Don't move,' said the harsh, unreal voice from behind the stranger's grotesquely masked face. But the uniform man kept on rising from the seat, going against the gun armed only with courage and a piece of polished wood.

'I don't want to shoot. But I will. Get back.'

The words tumbled over one another, broken in tone, the gun wavered, as, babbling his warnings, Renfield felt a sudden choking feeling in his chest. The policeman came on.

Panic-stricken at this crazy menace to his plans, the gun grown suddenly large and heavy in his hand, Renfield shot, shot to kill, to remove this threatening obstacle which blinded him to all reason.

Then he took the money and escaped.

CHAPTER SIX

SITTING IN THE CAR NOW, driving away, the thought of that awful moment and its full implications hit him for the first time. He moaned softly, half-shutting his eyes, then jerked back to reality as he had to brake fiercely to avoid hitting the back of a tramcar which had halted at a stop to allow two children to alight.

'Watch where you're going, you fool,' howled the tram conductor, shaking his fist from the platform, while the frightened children sprinted for the pavement.

From then until the safety of the lock-up he kept his attention rigidly on the road.

Finally, he reached his destination, opened the lock-up doors, drove the car inside, shut the doors again, and returned to sit in the silent vehicle. Slumped there, suddenly exhausted, he felt terror flooding through him in shivering waves which extended from his knees to his fingertips.

The bag... the bag with the money. That was the antidote.

The bag was held shut by a small but strong brass lock. Fetching a heavy screwdriver from his tool-kit, he forced the tip of the blade between the two metal edges, and face contorting with the effort, tried to lever them apart.

At the fourth attempt the lock was forced, the lips of the bag swung apart. A gasp escaped him as he saw the packed bundles of banknotes, all neatly held by rubber bands, just as they had been prepared by the bank staff.

Softly he shut the bag and replaced it on the car seat.

The next job was to unload the motorcycle from the rear of the shooting brake. Sweating at the effort, he stripped the canvas cover away, carefully lowered the machine out of the back doors, and placed the *Dot* neatly against the lock-up wall.

It took only minutes to unscrew the fake plates from the bike and substitute the genuine registration tabs, which he had stored under the driver's seat of the Ford.

Taking a glance at the bike's speedometer, he read the mileage.

"Only three miles more on the clock. Old Dawkins is too happy-go-lucky to ever notice a thing like that," he assured himself.

He peered closely at the motorcycle in the gloom. There were a few new scratches on the footrest and handlebar, a scrape on the mudguard and a smaller one on the fork. Nothing that would cause him any trouble to explain away.

All that remained to be done now was to hide the money. Going back to the car, he opened the bag again, and, taking out a bundle of pound notes the size of a small loaf of bread, stripped a folded wad from its bulk, a wad containing about fifty pounds. Stuffing the money into his pocket, he returned the main bundle to the bag, then wrapped the battered leather container and its contents in an old, torn plastic raincoat.

The lock-up was one of three erected by a hopeful mechanic who, starting out on his own, had sunk his savings and gratuity into war surplus equipment, the huts, and two old lorries.

The business, like many others of its kind, had failed. The huts had become the property of a local builder and were now used solely as lock-ups. Renfield's Nissen, like the others, had a scanty ash floor on top of bare earth. It didn't take long, using his hands and a tyre lever, to scrape away a hole big enough to take the bundle.

Then he replaced the earth, covered the brown patch with ashes, and carefully dispersed the surplus earth over the rest of the floor, stirring the ashes with his feet until no trace could be seen. Closing and locking the garage door behind him, Renfield set off at a brisk pace through the gathering dusk, heading for his lodgings.

Ten minutes later Mrs Bessie Senior was just setting the table for tea in her home at 14 Woodcraig Drive when she heard the front door open and her lodger's cheery voice call, 'I'm back, Mrs S... ready for tea. I've just been out for a run in the car.'

She went back to the kitchen, and a little later returned with a plate of home-made scones for the table.

At that exact moment her lodger was busy burning the flesh-coloured false face in the grate. Crushed, crumpled, he had torn it from his face and stuffed it into his coat pocket seconds after his bike had disappeared from the sight of the Rolls' chauffeur.

The material flared, was consumed, and died. Renfield stirred the last ashes to dust and tried to forget—forget the bewildered look on a dying man's face.

CHAPTER SEVEN

CHIEF DETECTIVE INSPECTOR COLIN THANE, head of the Criminal Investigation Department in the Millside Division of Glasgow police, was, for once, relaxed behind his big wooden desk.

One leg draped over an arm of the swivel chair, exposing an expanse of home-knitted sock, he was studying a copy of a "do it yourself" magazine; subject, how to paper a ceiling, and translating the instructions into personal terms of tears and sweat. The telephone rang.

With a sigh he marked his page with an old message pad form, swung his leg off the chair arm, and lifted the receiver.

'999 message, sir,' the voice of the duty officer at the bar, the C.I.D. outer office, came tumbling over the wire. 'Someone's got away with the Swivney factory payroll. A masked motorcyclist shot and killed the uniform man escorting the car and escaped with about seven thousand pounds.'

Galvanised to life, Thane fired questions to the duty man.

'The hold-up was in Scrutton Street, sir, about five minutes ago,' he was told. 'A lorryman has just phoned in. He says the other two men in the car are unhurt, but that the constable's dead.

'The chauffeur managed to note the motorcycle's number and passed it to the lorryman.'

'Have a car brought round for me immediately,' said Thane. 'I'll go there at once. Put out the motorcycle number and all other details over the teleprinter network. I suppose the radio is already giving it to all cars? Good. Have we any cars in the area yet?'

'There's a C.I.D. car on its way now, sir. Detective Sergeant MacLean was out on a housebreaking inquiry. We've switched him. A couple of patrol cars have already arrived,' replied the duty officer. 'Will I get the Scientific Bureau men at Headquarters to turn out?'

'Yes, do that,' agreed Thane. 'And get hold of the police surgeon. Then ask the uniform side to send a van-load of men out to cordon off the hold-up area and push any more cars you can get over to that direction. Oh, and you'd better get the motorcycle description circulated to the neighbouring county forces, on the chance our man has got clean away from the city.'

Thane put down the phone, a familiar dry, tense feeling in his throat.

Shoving the magazine into the top drawer of his desk, he stood up, reaching for his hat and coat, and shouting as he did so to his Detective Inspector, Philip Moss. Moss was in his tiny office next door, separated from the C.D.I's room by a thin wallboard panelling.

'Come on, Phil, panic stations. Some motorcycle bandit murdered one of our lads and got away with a lot of money. There's a car coming round.'

There was a curse, muffled by the partition wall, the

scraping back of a chair, and Moss, small for a policeman but wiry, coat shrugging onto his narrow shoulders, joined him.

Thane, consulting the big map of his division spread on one wall of his room, pointed a long, broad finger.

'It's the Swivney payroll. The car was on its way back from the bank with the money for tomorrow's wages. It was jumped just about here. Right in the middle of factoryland. I knew this would happen someday.'

'Right, Colin,' affirmed Moss. 'Ready when you are. Oh... hold on. I'll be right back.'

He dived into his room again and emerged clutching a small bottle in one hand and stuffing a pillbox into his coat pocket with the other.

'Just in case it's a long job,' he explained. 'Got to look after my duodenal.'

'That ulcer of yours,' sighed Thane, shaking his head. 'What's the latest witch's brew you're trying?'

'Olive oil and vitamin C tablets,' explained Moss, as the two men walked along the corridor, belting up their coats as they went. 'A fellow I know got the tip from a friend of his. Can't fail, he says.'

'Just like the others,' agreed Thane. 'You'll soon need another filing cabinet in your room to store all your cures.'

They clattered down the stairway, hastened along the hall past the "uniform" section of the police office and the cells which led off it, and went out into the courtyard.

A big black Austin was waiting at the doorway. The two men had no sooner piled aboard than the blue-coated driver started the engine, put the car into gear, and let the clutch bang home with a jerk that sent the Austin flying forward.

'Cut in the siren,' ordered Thane. At a flick of a switch the high-pitched piercing wail, a herald of emergency heard only rarely in the city, began its warning howl as the car nipped through the traffic at a rate which ignored all speed restrictions.

Thane had switched on the car's two-way radio. After the first sputterings had settled to a steady crackling hiss, he picked up the hand-mike.

'Car 26, Chief Inspector Thane, we're on our way to Scrutton Street—over,' he called. From the distant radio nerve centre, Control replied, 'Roger 26. We have five cars in attendance, plus ambulance. Search is in progress.'

In the rear seat, Moss gazed grimly ahead as Thane replaced the instrument under the dashboard.

Policemen usually deliberately cultivated an outwardly impersonal air towards violence, even death. They came too close, found it all too commonplace, to allow themselves to wallow in normal emotional reactions of hate or fear, pity or distress. But the thin protective mental curtain, a curtain essential to preserve a steady, unbiassed balance, was considerably torn when it came to cop-killing.

Cops—polis—bobbies—rozzers... they seemed too often to the outsider to be mere law-enforcing machines. But they had their families, friends, homes, just like everyone else. Their uniform had no special magic when it came to their being hurt or killed.

He glanced at Thane. Young for a C.D.I. at 43, a man who had broken a run of big cases in brilliant fashion, Thane was tall, dark, clean shaven and a trifle plump. But he still retained the powerful physique which had in earlier years made him an outstanding athlete.

Married, with two children, the Chief Inspector lived in a little bungalow in Southwood, where he loved nothing better than digging his pocket-sized garden.

He didn't drink, he smoked too much. He was, in fact, a reasonable picture of a suburban family man in many ways.

But the set of his shoulders, his air of quiet, assured authority, marked him separate.

As if realizing his appraisal. Thane half-turned, then, holding to the lip of the dash as the big black car rushed a corner in a scream of rubber, said, 'Looks like a tough one. Unless we get this man before he goes to cover it may be a long job. These one-man-band efforts...' he shook his head.

Moss, nodding agreement, said, 'It's always worse when there's only one. If there's a gang, more people know what's going on, there's always the chance of a split.' He asked, 'Who was the lad we had on the car?'

'A boy called Macrae. A nice lad, you know, Highland background. His father was in the police too... died a couple of years back after being on pension for a while. Family come from Lewis way, I believe.

'He was a promising young fellow. Keen on sport too—I've seen him playing in the Division football team. And now some gun-happy bastard is on the loose with seven thousand in his hand and Macrae's death chalked up against him.'

'I knew him,' said Moss. 'Macrae, that's the fellow who caught that razor slasher a few months back. It took some guts, too, if I remember. The slasher was fighting drunk and had given two people the "message" before Macrae nailed him.'

Dropping a gear to accelerate past a string of tramcars, the driver chipped in, 'That's him, sir. Ewan Macrae was his name. Engaged to a girl at Headquarters, too. One of the typists, I think.'

The car shot across a junction, waved on by a points policeman, who had stopped all other traffic on hearing the siren.

The driver eased the wheel over to pass a lorry, and asked, 'What's the chances, sir?'

Thane sat silent for a moment, eyes watching the buildings

flicker past, before he replied. 'Too early to say. But this one we must get. Once a man uses a gun it becomes a habit. He's got to be nailed quickly in case he tries it again.'

Control was feeding fresh positioning instructions to the squad cars as the Austin, rounding the last curve in the road, came within sight of its goal.

The Rolls' outline stood out amid a gaggle of sleek police cars, a brown-coloured ambulance sitting a little way off.

Police who were keeping a small crowd of gaping pedestrians back from the area cleared a way through them to allow the Austin to glide up beside its fellows.

As the car halted, a detective sergeant, one of several C.I.D. men already on the spot, came over.

'Hello, sir. Glad to see you. It's a bad one, I'm afraid. Young Macrae's body is untouched beside the car, though he was moved by the other occupants at the time of the shooting to see if they could help him.

'The cashier and chauffeur are unhurt, as you know. They are with Detective Constable Findlay in one of our cars.

'Both say they can't give a description of the man at all. Just medium height and build, dark-haired, dressed in an old raincoat... the swine was wearing a false face. Faked an accident, then shot two of the car's tyres when they halted.

'The cashier's a decent type. He doesn't seem to give a damn about the money. Just keeps talking about the murder. Dose of shock, I think.'

'A false face? What in—?' exclaimed his chief. Then, comprehending, 'Hallowe'en time. It's Hallowe'en time tomorrow, and it would be so darned simple to buy any number of Hallowe'en masks in the shops without being remembered. I got two myself in *Woolworths* the other day to take home to the kids.

'How about the motorcycle? Any luck?'

The sergeant shook his head. 'No trace at all, sir. It just seems to have vanished.'

Thane turned to Moss, waiting at his elbow. 'Check on the radio that the Scientific Bureau people are on their way. The doctor should arrive in a couple of minutes. You know the drill, Phil. And get the whole area cordoned off. We may need every wisp of evidence we can get, and I don't want a horde of sight-seers trampling over the place.

'From the look of the street, I don't suppose a soul saw or heard anything useful. But there are lord knows how many men employed behind these brick walls. There is just a chance.'

Moss, nodding, stepped quickly away, leaving Thane to walk slowly over the road towards the silent limousine, where a single constable stood guard.

A blanket from the ambulance had been draped over the body which, one shoe projecting, still lay in the shadow of the opened car door.

The detective slowly lifted a corner of the cloth and gazed at the huddled figure beneath. A small pool of blood had formed to one side. Two young blue eyes stared lifelessly skywards.

'Just leave it, Colin,' spoke a gentle voice at his side. The police surgeon had arrived. 'I won't move anything until the lab people have finished, though there's really nothing for me until the post-mortem. I've asked for the "shell" to be sent over.'

The shell, a plain wooden coffin, would remove the body to the City Mortuary, where the forensic experts would carry out their grisly tasks.

No matter how obvious the cause of death, a full report must be made, establishing physical condition of the body, the nature of the death-wound, and details which could include such things as how far away the gun had actually been when fired.

The Scientific Bureau men, laden with equipment, were just arriving in their radio van when Moss reappeared.

He reported that he had put a man at each end of the lane from which the masked rider had emerged, giving strict orders to allow no one through. The crowd in the roadway had been pushed still further back, well clear of the area.

'I've had the road closed to through traffic. They're all being diverted about a quarter-mile down the road on either side. We've had no luck with witnesses, though. A couple of men in the yard over the wall there heard the sound of shots being fired and the commotion that followed. But they didn't see anything.

'A message has come over the blower from Control, Colin. The Traffic Department have checked with the licensing people. The registration number's a fake. The original number belongs to a Corporation bus. That rules out a stolen bike. This machine was prepared for the job.'

Thane agreed. It at any rate appeared to rule out a machine "borrowed" that day and deprived him of one more chance of getting a quick lead.

Pushing his grey, soft hat back on his head, he declared, 'He's away, Phil. Half an hour's clear start he has had by now. We need a break, badly.'

Detective Sergeant MacLean, coming towards them, asked, 'Would you like to see the cashier and chauffeur now, sir?'

Thane glanced up at the darkening, cloud-filled sky, now being lit by occasional flashes as the police photographer began recording the murder setting from every angle and shook his head.

'They'll need to wait a bit yet. You've got a man taking a preliminary statement from them?'

MacLean told him that this was being done. 'The cashier's wondering about his firm, though. He suggested that he might be allowed to contact them so that some arrangement could be made to get another load of money out to them so that they can pay their workers as usual tomorrow morning. It seems it takes a bit of time to make up the wage packets.'

'Tell him we've more important things to... Oh, all right. Say we'll contact the firm, and that a police car will run a fresh consignment of money from the bank, if Swivneys give the authorization. Contact the firm yourself and make the necessary arrangements.'

Over at the Rolls Royce, a fingerprint expert was blowing a white powder from a little spray onto the doors. He looked up as the Millside chief's tall figure approached.

'A lot of prints here, sir,' he declared. 'But I understand the gunman wore gloves. Still, there are a couple of smudges here which he may have left, and even if they are just glove marks, we might learn something from the pattern.'

'I've a job for the rest of your gang,' said Thane. 'I want the place where the motorcycle fell examined in detail, the tarmacadam checked for paint scrapings, anything like that.

'In case we aren't finished in time, I'll get some portable floodlights sent out. And right now, I'll get every available man to start a step-by-step search of the area, on the off-chance that there's anything lying about which might help us. I'm not suggesting he's left his name and address on a visiting card, but there might be some trace.'

He shouted to a uniform constable, who came trotting over. 'Stand over at the spot where the motorcycle came down... just about there. Keep everybody off it, I don't care who he is, until the Scientific Bureau men are ready to examine it.'

Leaving their cars parked as closely as possible to the police cordon, a new group of men arrived on the scene, hurrying through the crowd. Reporters and photographers, their offices having been alerted by a "tip off" telephone call made to each in turn by the proprietor of the dairy where the 999 call had been made by the lorry driver.

The dairyman had a friend in the newspaper business, and knew that his information, if passed quickly, would be snapped up and that the newspapers would pay him well for his trouble.

The irresistible force of pressmen met an immovable object in the shape of the police cordon, and after a few seconds of heated argument, a detective constable brought word to Thane that the pressmen were seeking an official statement.

'They can damn well wait, I've got work to do,' he snapped. 'Tell them I'll give them something later. Make it half an hour.'

The news photographers, their electronic flashguns working from outside the cordon, gave further proof of the gathering darkness. The reporters, having rapidly sifted through the bystanders, swarmed round the only one who seemed able to tell anything about what had happened, the mufflered lorryman. They plied him with questions and suggestions as he told his tale.

Then the evening paper men among their number faded back to their cars, scribbling furiously in their notebooks. There was, they cheerfully remarked, just nice time to catch the last edition. It was a pity though that the photographers hadn't a chance of their pictures making the papers that evening.

'David Renfield will just about blow his top when he hears about this,' said a young Evening View reporter to his driver, as he roughed out an introduction to his story. 'There he is, our walking crime encyclopaedia, and every time anything decent happens he is on day off.'

Calling up his office on the radio, he began to dictate: '"A young policeman was shot down in cold blood today." No, kill that. We'll try this instead. "An unarmed Glasgow policeman was murdered by a motorcycle gunman in Millside this afternoon when a seven thousand pound factory payroll car was held up and robbed." Stop, new par.

'"One of the biggest police hunts in years is now in progress. An early arrest is expected..." What's that?'

The radio speaker croaked a question from the distant office.

He answered, 'No, I don't know whether they'll get anybody for it. But Thane's in charge, and he doesn't let the grass grow under him. Besides, I've a pretty lean story, and I need all the padding I can raise.'

CHAPTER EIGHT

PROBING, searching, checking, questioning, Thane, Moss and their murder squad men had no rest that night.

The search for the motorcycle, a seemingly hopeless but necessary procedure, continued. Battery-powered floodlights burned long into the darkness as the lane and roadway were examined. The Rolls Royce was finally removed after some hours, two new wheels attached. The car was taken straight to Headquarters garage, for a more detailed examination, the bullet-punctured wheels going to the laboratory for the extraction of the metal slugs.

Thane gave orders for the lane to remain sealed and for a second examination of it to be made at daylight the next day. Finally, driven back to Millside Police Station about 7 p.m., he had a quick cup of tea and a cold meat sandwich, then asked for the cashier and chauffeur to be shown in one at a time.

He just managed a glance through the cashier's statement before the man was ushered in. William Mertoun, head cashier at Swivney's Engineering Factory, was fifty-nine years of age, and had been with his firm from the days when he was a junior clerk.

Patiently, Thane once more led him through his story of the robbery, hoping for the chance word which might lead to a point not already known.

Only one new fact emerged. Mertoun, telling of the stranger's warnings, said, 'You know, he didn't have the sort of voice I'd expect a crook to have. Of course, it was muffled through the mask, but I'd swear that, whoever he was, he was an educated man. Oh, he was a Scot, all right. But it wasn't a Glasgow accent. And he was frightened. I'm sure of that.'

'What makes you think that, Mr Mertoun?' asked Thane.

'Just his attitude... even before he shot the policeman. I just can't describe my reasons, but I'm sure he was nearly as terrified as I was.'

He plunged on, 'I know it seems criminally stupid now, Mr Thane, but we just never thought of a robbery. Why, for about ten years now I've gone to the bank by car every Thursday afternoon. It was just the custom. My predecessor carried out the same routine... and the road we went along seemed so quiet and peaceful.

'That young policeman—Mr Macrae was his name, wasn't it...' he halted, running his tongue over his lips in a nervous movement. 'Well, he seemed a bit worried the first time he came with us as escort, but, well, I thought he was just being over-enthusiastic, a keen young man...'

He lapsed into embarrassed silence.

'It is too late now for me to say how damn silly your firm's security ideas were, Mr Mertoun. Perhaps we should have been more insistent on change. But you can console yourself with the thought that about three-quarters of the firms in the City of Glasgow are careless when it comes to moving money.'

Thane's voice was gruff but kindly, as he realised that the older man was on the verge of tears.

'What does matter now is that one of our men is lying in the mortuary beside Glasgow Green, and that your firm's payroll has gone. Our job is to do everything we can to catch the man responsible. To start with, tell me how the money was made up.'

The cashier grimaced. 'That's one of the worst bits. There was five hundred pounds in brand new ten-shilling notes. They had just been delivered as part of a large consignment at the bank this morning, so the bank people should know their numbers. But the rest, one thousand pounds in one-pound notes, five thousand pounds in five-pound notes, and about five hundred pounds in twenty-pound notes, was just made up in bundles of used notes. I don't imagine the bank people will be able to tell you anything about them. It's only on very rare occasions. Chief Inspector, that banks bother about such things as serial numbers. They haven't got the time.

'As you know, of course, the man ignored the canvas bags I had in the car. They contained about two hundred pounds in silver.'

'That tallies with our information,' agreed Thane. 'I sent a man along with the squad car which picked up the substitute package of money, and he stayed behind to check on the make-up of the original draft.

'Purely as a matter of routine, Mr Mertoun, would you give me a list of your assistants at Swivneys—people who might either handle the money, or who would do this collecting job?' asked the detective, pushing a piece of paper and a pencil towards the cashier.

Mertoun raised an expressive eyebrow, but, after a moment's thought, scribbled busily, then handed the list to Thane without comment.

'That's all just now, Mr Mertoun. But if you remember anything, anything at all, which you haven't already mentioned, contact me immediately. It may be something which doesn't seem important to you, but it may be vital to us.'

The chauffeur, George Weybridge, a middle-aged man, was next to come into the room. He sat down in the chair opposite Thane, twisting his peak cap in his hands.

'I was scared stiff,' he admitted. 'I just couldn't think of anything except that it might be me next. I wasn't going to be a ruddy hero. No—I didn't mean that...' He flushed. 'But I've got a wife and family, and, well, it wasn't my money, sir.'

Thane nodded sympathetically, though at the same time, the bitter thought came to him that it hadn't been the dead man's money either. But then, that was what policemen were for, to be "ruddy heroes." If they were shot, their dependents would always get a few shillings a week pension from a grateful public.

'Is there anything else you can remember, anything about the raid that isn't in here?' he asked, pointing towards the typed transcript of the chauffeur's earlier statements.

'Nothing sir... that is, except for the fact that this ruddy killer knew his motorcycles. I've got a boy of my own who is motorbike daft. And believe me, looking back, only a real expert could have pulled the trick he did without smashing up that bike.'

'You haven't noticed anything unusual these last few weeks? Anybody following the car, or asking questions?' queried Thane.

The chauffeur shook his head. Everything had been as normal.

'How many people knew of the route you took?' persisted the detective.

Weybridge bristled. 'Look, mister. If you're trying to suggest that I had anything to do with this, you're barking up the wrong tree. I've got a good job, a happy home, and enough to get by on. And I don't shoot my mouth off to strangers.'

Thane silenced him with a wave of his hand. 'I'm sorry, Weybridge. I've got a job to do. What I meant was does anybody else ever drive the car? What happens when you're on holiday, or sick?'

Mollified, the driver explained, 'One of the firm's lorry drivers takes over. But they're a decent bunch of lads. They wouldn't do anything like this.'

'Maybe not,' said Thane. 'But perhaps they told somebody sometime. Maybe they had too much to drink one night at the pub or wanted to impress a pal or their best girl. A policeman's got to have a dirty, suspicious mind, Weybridge.'

He sighed as the chauffeur left. Then, as Moss came into the room, he brightened once more. 'Hello Phil, how's the guts getting on?'

'Awful,' said Moss. 'That damn fool orderly brought me a sandwich made of the fattiest cold meat you ever saw. It's been burning a hole through me ever since. Leave me to my agony. How did the interviews go?'

'Pretty much of a dead loss, Phil,' said Thane, as the inspector sat opposite him and offered a cigarette. 'Still, we'd better get down to it. Run the rule over both Mertoun and Weybridge, though make it as inconspicuous as possible. While you are about it, put a man on to finding out something about the other drivers at Swivneys. And here's a list of Mertoun's assistants, the only other people with any real knowledge of what goes on when the money's picked up. This looks rather like an inside job at the moment, or an inside-aided job.

'Don't make that too obvious, though, in the inquiries. I don't want the Swivney bosses purging their staff because of groundless suspicion.

'Then we'll have to see what the laboratory boys have to tell us. After that, you and I are going to have a session in the Modus Operandi Department's files.'

'Looking for thugs who ride motorbikes?' asked Moss.

'Exactly,' agreed his chief. Thane was pinning a lot of hope on these two backroom departments. In Glasgow's resources, he had at his disposal an organization which he regarded as second to none in Britain.

The Scientific Branch specialists had qualifications ranging from such obscure skills as being able to identify at a glance different manufacturers of string, to the ability to handle the most up-to-date laboratory apparatus with all its analytical possibilities.

They had, on one occasion, identified a man and secured his conviction purely on the evidence of a tiny piece of cut skin he had left behind on a broken window.

The Modus Operandi and Criminal Records Office had on file details of nearly 300,000 people whose activities at one time or another had attracted the attention of the police.

Fifty thousand photographs, 125,000 sets of fingerprints, were contained in their tall metal filing cabinets. But more important still, when an unknown man was being hunted, the Modus Operandi Department had their "customers" cross-indexed under their habits, their descriptions, the types of crime they specialised in, and any skills, legal or illegal, they possessed.

Between them, these two departments brought to book

hundreds of wanted men each year. Would they, he wondered, once more succeed?

The two men rose from their chairs, ready to begin their tasks. 'Oh, oh, I nearly forgot,' said Thane. 'I haven't telephoned Mary yet. One thing about a bachelor like you, Phil. No wife to worry about when you stay out late.'

'Don't cry for me,' grunted Moss. 'I get the best of both worlds. Your wife's the only woman I've met who can cook me a meal that won't start my ulcer throbbing, and she'll never turn a starving man away. I can be a nice uncle to your kids... but I can nip along to the pub when I like, or go for a game of golf, and the landlady doesn't mind as long as I pay my rent.

'You, by comparison, are henpecked, Mr Chief Inspector.'

Thane waved a friendly, threatening paw, then lifted the phone and got the switchboard operator downstairs to ring his home. There was a resigned note in his wife's voice when she answered.

'I'm sorry, dear,' he told her. 'I'll have to keep working on this murder. What... Yes, I'll get a couple of hours' sleep on the camp bed in the office. Sorry I can't manage home. Yes, I'll phone in the morning. Give my love to the kids.'

CHAPTER NINE

BEHIND A CHEERY, whistling front, David Renfield was strained to near breaking point. He forced himself to eat the substantial liver and bacon tea laid before him by his landlady.

He teased her about the elderly bachelor living along the road "who's just gasping to marry a good-looking widow like you," then pretended to relax behind the evening paper.

Relax? He read and re-read, sifting and analysing every word of the payroll robbery story, which was almost jumping from the front page in its abundance of black type—a type which, the newspaper staff declared, was normally reserved for stories of the "bottom falls out of universe" calibre.

It was a hasty, threadbare account, hurriedly scraped together, then "padded" with phrases to disguise the lack of information available. The policeman had been "brutally, callously slain," and the other two occupants had "escaped by a miracle."

A man had even been found who, for the sake of seeing his name in print, was willing to declare that, despite the fact that he had seen nothing and had been separated by a couple of buildings from the roadway, had heard the sound of "a hail of bullets" being fired.

The noise of the telephone ringing in the hallway jerked him upright in his chair. Mrs Senior opened the door a moment later.

'It's the office, Mr Renfield,' she said. Then, noticing his white, strained expression, 'Is anything wrong?'

'No, no, nothing's wrong, Mrs Senior. I was just dozing off and was a bit startled,' said Renfield, slipping past her into the hall. 'I expect it's just some query or other they want answered.'

The news editor's voice, metallic over the wires, answered his hesitant 'Renfield here.'

'Sorry to trouble you on your day off, David,' crackled McRowder's voice. 'You'll have heard about this payroll murder. Well, I want you to get straight onto it in the morning. Thane's holding a press conference at Millside Police Station at 10 a.m. Have a scout around the area first, then go to the station. I'll have a radio car with photographer pick you up at your lodgings at eight. Unless they pull in someone overnight and the mornings get first bite at the cherry, this'll be the splash for certain, so build it up.

'Incidentally, how's that girlfriend of yours? Jean, that's her name, isn't it? If I were ten years younger...' a low, expressive growl came through the phone. 'Seeing her tonight?'

The wallpaper pattern, a hideous Regency stripe, had suddenly begun to waver before Renfield's eyes. This was the final trump card he had hoped for, almost certain the assignment would be his. Cover the murder hunt! Chart for hundreds of thousands of people the progress of the police in a search in which he was the hunted man!

'David... you there...?' the phone crackled impatiently.

'Yes, yes, right, I'll do that, Mr McRowder,' he stammered.

'Yes, I'm seeing Jean tonight. In about an hour in fact. I'll get in touch with you early tomorrow. Good night.'

He hung up and turned away, sweat breaking on his forehead.

Cover his own crime! He had realised that as "police calls" man on the View reporting staff, the hold-up was almost automatically his pigeon.

An ironic smile touched his lips as he considered the position. The possibilities of the situation were as valuable as they were fantastic, just as long as he kept his head.

He would be close to the hub of the hunt. Thane, if not a friend, was at least a familiar acquaintance who not only sometimes hitched a lift into town from his home nearby in Renfield's car, but occasionally gave off-the-record hints which had more than once steered the reporter towards an exclusive story.

For the first time since the picture of the shot policeman's slumped body had etched itself into his mind, he felt a little happier. But now he'd have to move if he was going to be on time at Jean's home. The date was part of the plan, which called for no departure from normal.

Hustling up the stairs, the reporter washed and shaved, then changed into his blue double-breasted suit and a clean white shirt, whistling as he wove a Windsor knot into his dark red tie.

"Every inch the gentleman, David," he assured himself, glancing into the mirror. "Nothing of the motorcycle bandit about you now."

He was still whistling when, a few minutes later, he entered the lock-up garage to take out his car.

The tune died away as he saw the motorcycle propped against the wall and the now covered-up spot where the money was buried. But the same tune was humming in his mind again when, exactly at 7.30 p.m., he turned his car into Atlight Road and drew up outside the entrance at No. 165.

It was what Glasgow calls a "wallie close"—tiled, clean, neat, voicing a respectability which shuddered at the soot-stained stone and plaster poverty of its more down-at-heel tenement equivalents in other parts of the city.

Jean's parents stayed in a six-apartment flat one stair up, behind a door with a coloured glass window and a sparkling brass nameplate.

It opened promptly to his knock, and Mrs Catta, a thin, rather untidy woman, a cigarette dangling from her lips, waved him into the lounge.

'Jean will be ready in a minute, David,' she smiled, showing a mouthful of large, horse-like teeth. 'Just come in. She won't be long—if you're lucky. Well, you're looking very trim. I could take a shine to you myself.

'Would you like a drink while you're waiting? My husband's home... his night off, you know. The assistant's dealing with the usual queue of complaints down at the evening surgery, God bless him.'

As they entered the lounge she moved over to the sideboard and poured a glass of sherry for the visitor.

'Too true,' rumbled Doctor Catta's voice. 'And it is as good as any box of pills to have a few hours at my own fireside.'

Jean's father, pipe billowing a bright blue cloud of strong smoke, was sitting in a deep leather armchair carefully preparing a slice of tobacco, ready for his next fill.

'Sit down, lad, sit down,' he gestured towards a twin of his chair, placed at the other side of the blazing fire, and as Renfield thankfully sank into its cushioned comfort, went on, 'Well, isn't this a shocking business, this bobby getting shot? The man who did that should get a short walk and a long drop if there's any real justice. But if our blessed reformers could have their way he'd have a long holiday at the taxpayers' expense, and then come out to spend his pile.

'Tell me, now, do you know anything about the case at all? What's the inside information, eh? You news-hawks usually know more than can be printed.'

Despite the long hours John Catta had to work "feeding National Health prescriptions to my flock," as he put it, he filled any spare time left by digesting every "whodunit" novel he could lay his hands on. He never lost an opportunity to discuss a crime, the bloodier the better.

Sipping the sherry, Renfield explained, 'I'm on the story tomorrow, Doctor Catta. But I've been on holiday today, fixing up the car, and I've only read the stuff in the evening paper. Surely, though, you're not still in favour of capital punishment?' he went on, his voice edging slightly. 'How can any sane educated man support such a barbaric system?'

'Only putting the fear of death into the sort of thug running around Glasgow has prevented our having a ten times higher murder rate till now,' declared the doctor. 'The threat of a stout hemp rope's a better preventative than all your prison terms. And any doctor will tell you that prevention is better than cure.'

'The crime figures in other countries where the death penalty is abolished haven't shown any rise,' protested Renfield, adding more heatedly, 'Two wrongs don't make a right. And few criminals are the cut-and-dried rotters you soak up in all those books you read. There's a streak of wrongdoer in everybody's make-up.'

Jean's arrival saved the situation. She swept in, dark, almost Italian in appearance, a wide skirted, tight-waisted coat, with a scarf gay at the neck, showing her charm to perfection. A tiny hat perched on her glistening black mane of hair, which was tied in a deceptively casual ponytail.

They escaped to the car. Renfield could feel the wad of pound notes he had taken from the cashier's bag, burdening his hip pocket. But for tonight, at least, that money must remain untouched. He suggested, 'There's a good film on at the Odeon, Jean. Like to see it?'

But Jean had other ideas. 'We were at the cinema last time. David dear...' A purr. 'Take me along to Johnny Leslie's place. There's a party on tonight, and Carole, you know, the girl I knew at model school? She says we're invited.'

Normally the reporter would have made a determined effort to avoid such a "smart set" party, which not only involved the expense of taking along a couple of bottles to help lubricate proceedings, but usually ended with late-night supper in a robber's roost of a restaurant where prices were as expensive as the food was exotic and helpings were tiny.

But this night was different, he decided. It was no time for argument, rather a night to escape from reality. He smiled and, agreeing, 'Good as there, dear,' blipped the Ford's accelerator to produce a gay, sporting roar from the engine as they moved off.

It was nearly 2 a.m. when the car once more pulled to a rather unsteady halt outside 165 Atlight Road. The wad of notes was still intact in David Renfield's hip pocket, but his wallet was empty.

What a night! The thought of the murder hunt, the fear of discovery—all had vanished in the whirl of excitement. And then, at the end of it all, Jean, warm, passionate, had clung to him in the darkness of a quiet country road, her studied, cultivated languor discarded, her lips first soft, then hard and demanding.

A last, swift kiss in the car, then, as Jean disappeared into the close mouth, he drove away, whistling through his teeth.

There was what an onlooker could only have described as "a silly moonstruck smile" spread across his face as he put the car away for the night, eyes bright, mind a pleasant, woolly wonderland.

He still, however, had sufficient caution remaining to stuff the fake number-plates he had used on the motorcycle into the top of his trousers before he left the lock-up.

Minutes later, the wooden plaques burned bright on the dying coals in his room fire.

He was still happy as, after setting the alarm for 7 a.m., he dropped off to sleep. Nightmare figures did stalk the dark corners of his mind. But the hangover of physical exhilaration kept them well back, and there was a smile on his face as he remembered Jean's embrace.

CHAPTER TEN

IT WAS 3 a.m. before Colin Thane sank into the camp bed in the corner of his room to seize a few hours' rest. Eleven hours had passed since the 999 message which had set the manhunt in motion. And still there was not a single concrete lead in the murder hunt.

For nearly an hour he and Moss, aided by the Modus Operandi Department staff, had ploughed through the police files. From the multitude of crime dossiers, they selected a small exclusive company of "hard cases" whose records showed connections with motorcycling, guns, or big-time robbery.

Finally, Moss had departed with a preliminary batch of nearly thirty dossiers, with instructions to trace the men described and discover what they had been doing that afternoon.

The white-coated laboratory staff were hard at work when Thane looked in at their department high in the Police Headquarters building in St. Andrew's Street.

'Nothing yet, Colin,' Superintendent Nichols, head of the

police "boffin" section, told him. 'We'll send you a full report as soon as we can. But I'm afraid you'll need to give us more than you have so far before we can really be of much help.'

'We'll try, Mr Nichols, we'll try,' said Thane.

By then it was nearly 9.30 p.m. And the most unpleasant task of all waited him. He drove back to Millside station, collected the divisional superintendent, and they set off to visit the dead constable's home.

'His mother has already been told, of course,' said Superintendent Meddan. 'An inspector went out this afternoon, soon after we got the news. She took it pretty hard, though she tried not to show it. Young Macrae was her only son, you know.'

The car drew up outside a little council house block in Mosspark, and the two men scrunched up the gravel path towards the door. Mrs Macrae, red-eyed from weeping, but somehow, with struggling courage, maintaining a courteous air, opened the door as they approached.

She was a slight, still attractive woman in her early fifties. 'Come in, gentlemen,' she invited, and the two men, unhappily embarrassed, followed her into the tiny parlour of her home.

Clearing his throat, Superintendent Meddan said, 'Mrs Macrae, we've met before. And this is Chief Detective Inspector Thane, in charge of the Divisional C.I.D. I—*we*—we're terribly sorry about what has happened, Mrs Macrae. If it is any consolation to you, your son died a hero.'

'Thank you, Mr Meddan,' said the woman, her voice trembling. 'And thank you, Mr Thane, for coming along. Ewan often talked about you. He—he wanted to be a detective himself someday.'

She broke off, dabbing at her eyes.

'You must excuse me. The inspector who told me was kindness itself, but the shock was terrible.' She turned towards the old upright piano which stood against one wall of the room and lifted a photograph from its top.

'This was Ewan's father, Mr Thane. He was in the Force too. He was a sergeant with Mr Meddan at one time. And even when Ewan was little, he wanted to be a policeman like his father.'

The two men stood silent, not knowing what to say or do.

She went on, 'Ewan always worried about this money collecting he had to do on Thursdays. He told me once, "That big firm's awfully careless with its money. Fair gives me the willies, Mum." But he didn't like to say anything about it, him being in the police such a short time. If only my poor lad had, this might not have happened.'

'We'll do our best, Mrs Macrae,' said Thane, gently. 'Every man in or out of uniform is doing all he can. We'll find the man.'

The two men walked back from the little house with the drawn blinds, back to where the police car waited. Thane was thinking of the girl at Police Headquarters, the girl who had also wept, and who had asked only one thing: "They'll get him, won't they? They're bound to, aren't they?"

He slammed the car door savagely and turned to the Superintendent. 'Thank God that's over. That poor woman... You know, it beats me how anyone ever becomes a policeman. We ask them to risk their lives day after day—and give them a miserable pittance for doing it. Oh, I know, what is it the recruiting advertisements say— "Pay rises after six years' service to so much, and thereafter to a maximum of blank pounds." Top rates for some lucky beat constable after only fifteen years' service. And that's despite the fact that in education, fitness, height and heaven knows what else he is among the cream of the nation.

'No wonder that in the Glasgow Force alone we're

hundreds of men under strength. No wonder so many of the men that do join get out in record quick time. There's not a trade union in the land would allow its members to put up with the sort of conditions and risks that we ask the beat men to endure.'

'I know, Colin, I know,' agreed Meddan. 'But look at the other side of it. How many men in the Force do you know who could make better money in industry or business tomorrow if they wanted, but won't leave? There are hundreds, despite all the things you say. And why won't they leave? Because being a policeman is something more than just having a job.

'Oh, I'm not going to start flag-waving. But every man knows he's responsible for the continuance of law and order. And that means a lot to them. Just as much as it means to you. Don't glare at me. I know you had the chance of that big security post with the atomic energy people, and turned it down, even though it meant a darned sight bigger money. And I know why, just as well as you do.'

'All right,' Thane capitulated. 'You win. But I swear it, Super, this is one case that isn't going to end in an "incomplete" file, no matter how long it takes.'

Back at the police station, Thane found a note on his desk asking him to ring the Scientific Bureau. Despite the lateness of the hour, Nichols was still at the laboratory, and came to the telephone immediately.

'I've got the lab reports finalised, Colin,' he rumbled. 'Want to hear them?'

'Shoot,' said Thane, pencil in hand.

The Superintendent detailed his findings. The bullet which had killed the constable had been a seven-millimetre calibre, the alloy marking it as probably of German wartime manufacture. 'Which makes it any one of lord knows how many thousand guns smuggled over after the war,' he commented ruefully.

'Still, there are other things. Your hunch about where the machine fell has paid off. The marks on the road point to the bike being only scratched in the fall, which suggests an expert rider. And the paint scrapings from the tarmacadam show that the bike's colour was black, but had once been red. My lads are working on the actual paint now. Its chemical breakdown may enable them to name the make and possibly the year of manufacture of the bike, if the red paint was the original colour, which should be a help to you.

'We got a good set of tyre marks in the lane. The bike was a lightweight, tyres pretty well worn, a slight cut on one tread. Hmm... a cigarette end, ordinary make, means nothing. No prints on the car. False Face used gloves, probably woollen, according to the smudge on the door-handle. The pattern is perfectly ordinary, I'm afraid. There is no chance of further progress there. The only other thing to add is that the photographs are O.K. I'll send a set round in the morning with the written lab reports.'

Thane thanked the Headquarters man, replaced the telephone, then, lifting it again, asked the night duty operator, 'Any word from Inspector Moss?'

'He is out with one of the cars, Mr Thane,' replied the girl. 'The last we heard from him was about twenty minutes ago. He said he was still going through the motorcycle list.'

CHAPTER ELEVEN

AT THAT MOMENT MOSS, quietly munching one of the tea biscuits from the packet which he always kept in one pocket—"Keep giving your stomach something to work on," his doctor had once told him—was driving towards yet another address on the long list with which he had been supplied.

The car headed down through the Gorbals district, drawing suspicious glances from the groups of men standing at every corner, and finally halted outside a grey, crumbling tenement building.

As Moss and a plain clothes man entered the dark, ill-lit close mouth, the dank stench of dirt and poverty hit their nostrils.

'Watch your feet,' warned the inspector, and the two men began to climb the worn stone steps, past the dirty, glass-broken landing windows.

'Why do they always have to live on the top floor, sir?' panted his companion. 'This is the fourth in a row that has lived in the heights.'

'Tell me that, and you've solved one of the main mysteries

of the police force,' replied Moss. 'It always has been, and it always will be. If you want to talk to anybody in tenement land, he's sure to be at least three floors up. Phew... this is when I feel my age.'

They reached the top landing, and, by the faint light of the gas-jet, began to examine the doors that congregated round it.

'Here we are,' grunted Moss. 'Get a load of the fancy-work on the door. It's like a ruddy ice cream shop instead of a single end. Trust Danny O'Farrell to do himself proud. That last little job he pulled netted him a cool eight hundred quid, and we never found a penny of it.'

Flush-faced in shining, enamelled wood, boasting a tiny glass window set in the middle, the door had two handles, one a glass globe, the other like a miniature towel-rail.

"D. O'Farrell," said the tartan-backed name-plate beside the door-bell switch. Moss pressed the knob, and the sound of mellow chimes came from within.

Eyes peered through the glass, there was the sound of a chain being freed and a key turned in a lock. The door swung open, and a sly-looking young man of medium height, dark haired, dressed in shirt and trousers and in his stocking soles, stood in the entrance.

'Want a word with you, Danny,' said Moss, striding into the tiny hallway, the plain clothes man following.

'What you want with me, copper?' protested the man. 'You can't barge in like this.'

Ignoring him, the two policemen walked into the house's only room. A girl hurriedly shot to her feet from her chair beside the table, on which half a dozen bottles of beer and a couple of tumblers were laid on top of an old newspaper.

The room was a surprise in such a frowsy building. Walls neatly decorated, it had a television set and a radiogram fighting for supremacy in one corner. A fitted kitchen unit and an electric cooker replaced the normal worn black range and scarred sink. There were two deep armchairs, a bed-settee, a walnut sideboard with chromium-plated handles. Danny obviously believed in investing his money.

'Breaking up your party, chum?' inquired Moss. 'We won't take long. Where were you this afternoon?'

'What you want to know for?' snarled the girl, a tousled blonde in a black sweater and skirt. 'Throw them out, Danny.'

'He can't, love,' Moss told her. 'And you keep quiet till you're spoken to. Well, Danny? Still got that motorbike of yours? Had it out lately?'

Horrified comprehension dawned in O'Farrell's eyes. 'I'd nothing to do with it, Inspector, honest. You know me. I'll break into a house now and again, maybe get into a fight. But I've never used a gun in my life. I wasn't near the place where the copper was shot.'

'Where were you then, Danny? Out with it.'

'Along at the Labour Exchange, and I can prove it,' retorted O'Farrell. 'The bloke behind the counter had a real set-to with me. I can't get it into his thick head that I'm not fit for work. It's my chest.'

'Which Exchange? The one round the corner?' asked Moss. 'We'll check on that, Danny. I hope you're telling the truth for once, for your sake. Don't go too far from home till we find out, will you? Now we'll leave you and the lady friend in peace. Night night.'

Back in the squad car, Moss ran his pencil through yet another name on his list.

'Where to now, sir?' asked the driver.

'Back to the station,' sighed the inspector. 'I want to have a word with the boss.'

He found Thane scowling over a report form at his desk. A teleprinter check throughout the country had yielded no trace of any motorcycle having been reported stolen which might fit the hazy description available.

From the moment the bike had roared down the lane away from the crippled car it seemed to have been swallowed up.

'You know what that means, Phil. Somebody with his own bike, fitted with false plates,' pointed out the Chief Inspector. 'How's the suspect list going?'

'A blank so far. Panic and confusion when the subject of motorcycles is even mentioned, and a barrowful of alibis to be checked,' replied his assistant.

'I've had the word put round the grapevine,' said Thane. 'Absolutely nothing is known there.'

The network of police contacts—small shopkeepers in poorer districts, street bookies, publicans, even down-and-outs who hung around the fringe of the city's "wild men"—had been sounded during the night. But none had been able to help.

'Last hope tonight, Phil. Come on, we'll tap the coffee-stall crowds. I'll buy you a cuppa while we're there,' said Thane, rising. Groaning, Moss followed him out of the door, feeling in his pocket for another tea-biscuit.

They returned nearly an hour later, no further forward. The late-night coffee-stall clients, containing among their numbers many a hardened thug, thief and prostitute, drifter and drunk, were talking about little apart from the payroll murder.

But they were puzzled. And the less law-abiding were actually angry. The killing of a policeman meant only one thing to them, a tremendous comb-out which would without doubt uncover other matters best kept quiet.

CHAPTER TWELVE

IT WAS 7.30 a.m. when the sleepy-eyed Chief Inspector was wakened by a detective carrying a mug of tea and a couple of freshly-baked, still warm rolls. The collection of a batch of the latter was one of the unofficial tasks of the night duty car crew, whose patrol took them past a local bakery.

He was having a quick shave in the little washroom set off in one corner of the office when Philip Moss, also not long awake, came in.

'I've got the lab reports, Mr Thane,' he said. Then, duty to his superior done for the day, 'There's one or two more things tied up, Colin. All of the suspect list have been interviewed and seem to be in the clear. Their stories are being double-checked, of course. The back-shift men were pulling them out of their beds until about five this morning.'

Throughout the night, squads of detectives and uniform police from every division had raided homes throughout the city, and had questioned rudely awakened men whose records in crime marked them as suspect.

Nearly all had alibis, ranging from the man who had only

been released from Barlinnie, Glasgow's prison, late that afternoon, to the brothers who cited as their defence witnesses the sixty or so occupants of a bookmaker's shop where they had spent an unsuccessful afternoon betting on horse races.

'Mind you, they picked up Johnny Daniels at one house. He's wanted in Birmingham for a safe-blowing job, so we'll push him through the court today and get an escort sent up to collect him.

'As for Mertoun and Weybridge, they seem in the clear. Mertoun is as sound as a bell, no background troubles. The chauffeur has been up before the beak once, a breach of the peace on a Saturday night some twelve years ago. But he's all right otherwise. They haven't finished finding out about their pals yet, but that should be taken care of by noon.'

'Unless there's something there, that seems to dispose of the inside job angle for the moment,' shrugged Thane. 'Well, here's my idea for today's programme. We'll do another drag of the locals, try to trace that bike's route. Damn it, a motorcyclist with a leather bag dangling about him must have been noticed, even supposing he took that mask off the moment he turned into the lane.

'Then there is a particularly rotten job for the Traffic Department. I want a search started at the local Taxation Office. Every lightweight bike owner in Glasgow to be listed... No, we won't do anything with it yet. After all, the machine could have come from a county, or even England. But a list like that may be needed before we're done. Oh, and you could ask Scotland Yard for details of any likely candidates among their Criminal Records Office files. This might be an English job. The planning is good enough for some of the big-time thugs.'

Soon afterwards Thane took a car out on a quick visit to Mertoun's home, taking with him the bundle of photographs selected the previous night from the Records Office.

'Take a look at these, Mr Mertoun,' he requested. 'I know the gunman's face was covered, but there might be something in the set of a man's shoulders, even the shape of his ears, that might be familiar.'

The cashier, who had been at breakfast, sat long over the pictures. But he could spot nothing which stirred his memory.

'Thanks anyway, it was always worth trying,' said Thane. 'Don't trouble—I'll see myself out.'

He arrived back at the police station just after nine and was barely seated at his desk before the telephone rang.

'Bar officer here, sir. A reporter, Renfield of the View, here to see you.'

'Tell him the press conference is at ten,' snapped Thane.

'He knows that, sir,' explained the officer. 'He's got someone with him, a mechanic. Says the man may be able to help.'

Thane's voice changed. 'Oh. In that case, send him through till I find out what it's all about. But any other reporters that come along are told ten o'clock—unless they bring a body over each shoulder.'

Accompanied by a nervous young man in grease-stained overalls, David Renfield swung into the Chief Inspector's office a minute later, in high humour.

'Brought a lad along who may be able to help, Mr Thane,' he said. 'He saw your masked rider yesterday... without his mask.'

CHAPTER THIRTEEN

AS MCROWDER HAD PROMISED, the View radio car, with a driver and photographer, had pulled up outside Renfield's lodgings at exactly 8 a.m. Bill Gorebridge, the photographer, was still coming to life.

'All right for you, chum,' he yawned. 'But I didn't stop till midnight.'

Gorebridge had been on duty for the Bugle, the View's sister morning paper, and had been called in for this extra duty owing to a View rota man falling sick.

'I was still out on the tiles with Jean while you were snoring your fat head off,' boasted Renfield. 'I got in around 2.30 a.m.'

'Wow!' exclaimed Gorebridge. 'I don't know what a popsy like that sees in a slob like you. Strange tastes some women have.'

They continued their good-natured wrangling until they arrived at the factoryland street, now once more deserted apart from a trio of policemen, guarding the lane and the patch of roadway. Gorebridge took a picture of the scene, "just in case nothing better turns up." Then, driving slowly in the car, they detoured into the next street, the street which, about sixteen hours before, had been the scene of a desperate dash to freedom.

Renfield found two shopkeepers who remembered hearing the noise of a motorcycle passing. There was even a garrulous gatehouse keeper outside a factory who insisted that he had seen the rider, who was not only masked, but still had a gun clutched in one hand.

Then, just as he was about to turn back, he spotted the little garage, a corrugated iron structure which seemed held together solely by metal signs boosting the qualities of various petrol and oils.

The young, grease-blackened mechanic who slid from under an ancient lorry to answer his call gave him his story—and much more besides.

'Aye, sure I saw that bike. Going like the hammers, mister. Soon as the boss comes in, I'm going down to the police.' He knew the make of motorcycle. 'It was a *Dot*. A pal of mine has got one. The bloke on it, mister? Aye, I got a good look at him!'

Renfield's eyes widened, his face flushed. 'You saw his face? Would you recognise him again?'

'Aye, I think so,' affirmed the mechanic. 'Mind you, his head was down. But I got a good look at him. I'd say he was dark-haired, a bit bigger than you or me. An ordinary looking sort of bloke he was, too. But I'm sure I'd know him.'

The reporter's mind was in a whirl. He had come across the genuine article all right, a man who had seen him yesterday... a man who was convinced he could identify the rider, but who didn't know he was standing beside him.

It wasn't an uncommon situation. Witnesses often had only a quick glimpse of a man. Then, later, when they realised that what they had seen was important and tried to recall what he looked like, they built up a totally different picture without realizing their error.

The mechanic went on, 'He could handle that bike, mister. Took it round that corner there like the clappers, he did. That ruddy big bag there too—that would be the money, I suppose.'

'What time do you expect your boss to arrive?' asked Renfield, mind suddenly made up.

'Say fifteen minutes,' said the mechanic.

'Well, we'll come and give you a run along to the police station if you like,' offered the reporter, heart thumping. 'Now, what's your name?'

After the photographer had "dropped" a picture of the mechanic, one Jimmy Wheeler, posing self-consciously at the garage entrance, Renfield, promising to return, had the car driven round the corner.

He already knew what he would find—yet another nondescript stretch of roadway, flanked on one side by a high brick wall, on the other by iron railings flanking a school playground. Beyond them lay a small engineering yard, its wall pierced only by two wooden doors which gave entry for lorries.

At the foot of this short length of street was a busy tenement-lined road, used by trams, buses and all kinds of traffic, lined with shops. Yesterday, he had slowed his wild dash as he neared the main road and had stopped to pull on a pair of goggles and an old beret before steering quietly along it.

Now, a story-seeking reporter, he made a few brief inquiries at the shops. No, no one had noticed anything unusual. The trail had once more broken.

He went back for the mechanic.

CHAPTER FOURTEEN

'HE SAW our man did you say?' repeated Thane again.

'Aye, ah did,' said Wheeler. 'This reporter fellow said he'd bring me along to see you, mister.'

'Quite right too. This is grand, David,' said the policeman. 'Thanks a lot. Leave him to us now, will you?'

'Can I have a wee word with you first?' wheedled Renfield. 'After all, I found him.'

Thane's eyes narrowed, then he chuckled. 'Fair enough, I suppose you deserve it. But this once only... and not a word to the boys at the conference. They'd skin me if they knew the View man was getting a special dispensation.'

He pressed the buzzer on his desk, and a detective entered the room.

'Canvey, take this lad into the side room a minute, will you,' he ordered. As the mechanic was ushered out, Thane turned once more to the young reporter. 'All right, you young blackmailer, what do you want to know?' he grinned.

'How is the search going, Mr Thane? Any possible arrests in sight?' asked Renfield, carefully preparing his way.

'I'll know the answer to that more fully after I've had a word with your friend,' replied the policeman, offering his cigarette packet.

Taking one, and accepting a light, Renfield prodded, 'What can you say about the gun?'

'That's a fairly safe one. It was a seven-millimetre automatic... probably a wartime souvenir. We've got the bullets from the wheels and from Macrae's body, of course.

'Here's something for you. We were combing Glasgow all through the night, as you probably know. Now, don't quote me on any of this, but it looks as if this wasn't the work of any of the regular boys. And we actually picked up one man wanted for another offence. There's not much more I can really give at this stage.'

'One last point, Mr Thane,' pushed Renfield, fists clenched out of sight in his coat pockets. 'How about the money? Are the numbers of the notes known? How was the money made up?'

Thane frowned. 'David, you should know better than ask a daft question like that at this stage.

'Look, off the record, we've a chance there if the ten-shilling notes are unloaded. The rest, no. But I don't want to see a line of that in print, or even a hint, or...'

He raised his eyebrows expressively.

'Now let me get a hold of this lad you brought in. See you at ten—and mum's the word about this chat.'

By the end of the next half-hour a certain mechanic was beginning to wish he had never opened his mouth to anybody. Between them, Thane and Moss had dragged him over his story half a dozen times at least. Albums of photographs had been displayed before him with the plea, 'Can you see anyone there like the man?'

Wheeler found two men. One was currently in Peterhead,

doing five years for a hatchet assault. The other was Danny O'Farrell!

'Pick him up, Phil,' said Thane. 'Take some men with you. If he's our man, he may still be armed. We'll see how his Labour Exchange story stands up to this.'

Moss departed at top speed. Thane turned the mechanic over to a detective sergeant and constable, with instructions to obtain a full statement from him.

'You'll have to hang on a bit yet, I'm afraid,' he added. 'We're bringing in somebody we'd like you to have a look at.'

At 10 a.m. Thane walked down to the C.I.D. bar. Waiting him, as he had expected, were a crowd of reporters and photographers, eager young men, dress ranging from duffel coats to tightly belted Mackintoshes. Most of their faces were long since familiar.

Keeping a poker face, and mentally resolving to give no clue as to the startling development which had just taken place, he asked, 'Well, boys, what are you after?'

The questions flooded in. Had the gun been found? What about the motorcycle? How much money? Were there chances of an early arrest?

An English accent, desperate for a London angle, pleaded, 'Would you say the man is probably in England by now—have Scotland Yard been alerted, Chief Inspector?'

Thane, who had been trying hard to keep up with the flow, held up his hand. 'One at a time, for heaven's sake. Look, let's put it this way. Our investigations are continuing. We are anxious that anyone who saw a motorcyclist in the vicinity of the robbery area an hour in either direction comes forward immediately. If anyone knows of a motorcycle—a black motorcycle—which has been recently damaged, however slightly, let us know at once.'

Jock Mills, crime man for the Hour, rival organ to the

Evening View, cut in, 'How do you think he got away? And how about this false face? Have you had any luck tracing it?'

Thane shook his head. 'This is Hallowe'en, Jock. Mr False Face could have bought that mask anywhere. As for the route after the shooting, we've had some luck. But it is too early to say yet what's going to come of it.

'One thing you boys can print. Young Macrae's action in going for that gunman was one of the bravest things I've ever known. A lot of very important people feel the same thing, and word it carefully though, there may be a posthumous award of a medal.

'One other word. I want you boys to lay off the mother of the lad who was killed. If I catch a reporter or a photographer within a mile of Mrs Macrae I'll throw him inside and think of a charge later.'

He turned on his heel and walked away, while the pressmen, chatting among themselves, surged towards the exit from the police station.

'Lean, eh?' said Jock Mills' voice in Renfield's ear. 'I was hoping old Thane would give us a decent line. As it stands, this doesn't take us much beyond a rehash of the morning paper story. This suggestion of a medal is the only really new piece.'

Renfield nodded, but his eyes were bright. Mills caught the glitter.

'Say, Dave, got something special?' he asked, in a deceptively casual way. Then, offering a bait, 'I've got a nice little interview from a motorcycle club type saying just how difficult a stunt this rider pulled off.'

Renfield shook his head and jumped into the waiting View radio car. 'That wraps it up for now,' he told the driver. 'Back to the office, please.'

He sat back, story forgotten for the moment. The money was safe, all except the ten-shilling notes. He would destroy them. Only a fool would hang on to that sort of evidence, a greedy fool.

His heart seemed to tighten momentarily. Hang—a horrible word.

Then there was the fact that the police didn't know the escape route, and that by giving them a lead to a fragment of it he had ingratiated himself with Thane—and given him a witness who would muddle any identification attempts.

How many thieves, he wondered, had ever had the opportunity to ask the police "off the record" how they were getting on in their efforts to catch them?

The noon edition of the Evening View shouted: "View Man Aids Hunt for Mr False Face... Vital Witness located."

"By David Renfield," read the large-sized by-line under the heavy type.

CHAPTER FIFTEEN

DANNY O'FARRELL WASN'T at home when a squad of police poured out of cars and invaded the Gorbals tenement warren in which he lived. Neighbours insisted that he wasn't. But two brawny uniform men put their shoulders to his ornate door just to make sure... and Moss took a quick scout round the room.

There was no trace of the money, which came as little surprise. There was, however, a very interesting drawing in one drawer of the chromium-handled sideboard, showing the pencilled layout of a city centre public house.

It was complete with the location of the safe in a side office and a diagram of how a hole knocked through a wall from the cafe next door (to be entered through a skylight) would lead into the cocktail bar of the said pub.

'Aye, aye,' said Moss, 'Danny's getting careless. We'll take these with us. Now, I wonder where he's gone.' He turned to one of the local beat policemen who were helping in the swoop.

'Any ideas, son? Where do you normally find your local

neds about this time?'

The constable glanced at his wrist-watch. 'Too early for the pubs, sir. He'll be down at Slater the bookie's place. It is only a couple of streets away.'

'Lead on,' ordered Moss, and, leaving a couple of men to guard the forced door in case the safe-blower returned, the police squad piled back into the cars and headed towards the betting shop.

Their arrival in the shop—where about a score of men were already studying racing programmes, examining odds being offered, and preparing for the serious business of finding the winners on the day's card—caused only mild concern. The unwritten law of the bookmaking business is that in the event of a police visit all punters' fines are paid by the proprietor.

The irate boss of the establishment came forward protesting, 'It isn't my turn. I was raided last week. I've paid my fines. Away, and give someone else a shake-up.'

'Relax,' Moss assured him. 'We're merely collecting one of your customers.'

'Here he is, sir,' came a shout, and a detective emerged from the little washroom situated to one side of the cash desk, escorting a reluctant Danny.

O'Farrell stopped dead in his tracks when he saw Moss. Then he almost ran forward, dragging the detective with him.

'Mr Moss, I've got nothing to do with it. It wasn't me. I told you... I've never used a gun.'

'Keep your mouth shut, Danny. Nobody's said anything to you yet,' said Moss. 'I want you to come along to Millside with me. The boss wants to ask you a few questions. Be a good boy now, and it will be much easier for all concerned.'

The procession of police reformed, and, Moss leading, O'Farrell behind, pinioned by two detectives, marched out of the betting shop amid an awed silence from the punters.

In you get, Danny,' said Moss, opening the door of a police Humber. O'Farrell, a detective still on each side, slid into the seat, casting wild glances around.

'What's it all about?' he protested. 'I haven't done anything. Just because I've got a motorbike you can't hang a murder charge on me. For pity's sake tell me what's going on.'

The policemen sat silent, and O'Farrell, head sinking to his chest, remained still, a picture of abject misery, until the car halted in the courtyard of Millside Police Station.

Thane had just finished making a telephone report of the latest development direct to the Chief Constable when Moss marched in.

'Danny's waiting outside, Colin,' he said. 'Will I bring him in?'

'Yes, we'll give him the once-over,' agreed Thane. 'That mechanic, Wheeler, is still waiting in another room. One of the lads gave him a pile of old thriller magazines and he's quite happy. So, while you and I are asking Danny one or two questions, I'll get Sergeant MacLean to organise an identity parade.'

Lifting the telephone, he gave the necessary instructions, then, winking to his companion, picked up his pen and began scribbling on a sheet of paper before him. The door opened, and a detective announced, 'O'Farrell, sir,' then half-shoved the unfortunate individual into the room.

'Leave him,' ordered Moss, and the escort withdrew, leaving a bewildered, frightened crook standing alone.

Glancing round, O'Farrell saw Thane still writing, ignoring his existence, and Moss staring fixedly ahead.

'Giving me the treatment, eh?' he blustered. 'You can't do this to me. Send for my lawyer. I've got my rights, and fine you know it.'

Silence.

'You cops can't get anywhere on this payroll job, and so you think you'll hang it on me,' he tried again.

Putting down his pen and raising his head, Thane spoke for the first time. 'Isn't it strange, Inspector Moss, that people don't want us to hang murderers anymore,' he commented. 'Mind you, I don't imagine that even a long term in prison would be exactly fun, especially for someone with a cosy little house and a blonde—er—housekeeper to worry about.'

'What do you mean, murder,' whimpered O'Farrell, bluster disappearing. 'I haven't done anything. Ask the Labour Exchange people. They'll tell you where I was.'

Switching his gaze, Thane snapped, 'Danny, we want to ask you a few questions. First, of course, I've got to caution you that anything you say will be taken down in writing and may be used in evidence.

'Danny, we're investigating the murder of a police officer and the stealing of a large sum of money from a car. What do you know about it? You were in the infantry during the war. You know all about guns.

'Want to say anything about it to us, Danny?'

Moss, notebook poised, began scribbling furiously as O'Farrell, nervously running his hands over the lapels of his drape-cut suit, made in an allegedly Hollywood style cloth of near sky-blue, protested his innocence once more.

'Sure, I've got a motorbike. And maybe I sometimes have used it on little jobs. But you know me, Mr Thane. You've been pulling me in every now and then since I did my first term in Borstal. Have you ever known me to use a gun or a knife, or anything other than my fists?

'I've got a record. But I never used a weapon. I don't want to land before the High Court. I've told Mr Moss here already, I was at the Exchange.'

'Till when, Danny?' prompted Moss.

'Oh, I don't know. The bloke behind the counter kept me dangling on a string. I'm a citizen same as you, I told him, and you can't knock me around. They're as bad as the ruddy Gestapo, these deadheads.

'After I got out of that place, I just went a walk around the shops for a bit. I walked across the river and up to Argyle Street. No crime in that, is there?'

The telephone on Thane's desk tinkled to life. He lifted it and listened quietly to the voice on the other end, replying only an occasional cryptic 'Yes' or 'Are you sure?'

Finally, he replaced the receiver. 'Danny, you're in a spot. It will pay you to help us. Do you know anyone who can vouch for your movements after you left the Exchange—a shop assistant, anyone like that?'

'I can't think of anyone,' admitted O'Farrell. 'I just walked around the shops. I didn't buy anything on account of me not having much "ready" just now.'

'Was that why you were going to crack the pub safe, Danny?' asked Moss, gently. 'We found the drawing in your home.'

'Don't know what you're talking about,' glared the safeblower. 'If you found a drawing in my house it was just something I was telling the girl about the shocking way some of these places put temptation in people's paths.'

'Never mind that just now,' Thane pulled him back on to course. 'Where do you keep your motorbike? We want to take a look at it.'

O'Farrell mumbled the address, whereupon his inquisitor pressed the buzzer button, and, as the escort re-entered the room, instructed, 'Keep him somewhere by himself for a while. Don't let the mechanic get a glimpse of him.' A despondent Danny O'Farrell was led away.

Tapping his pen against his teeth, Thane stared into space

for a few seconds. 'That telephone call was from the man we sent to the Labour Exchange, Phil,' he finally announced. 'Danny was there yesterday afternoon. He left just about twenty to three. They remember him because of the row he kicked up.'

'Twenty to three? That would give him time to get out to hold up the car.'

'I know. But there's a lot of truth in what O'Farrell says, whether we like it or not. He's a slippery customer. But he's never been lifted with as much as a cosh in his pocket, even though he's over-handy with his fists.

'Oh, well, let's get the identity parade over. After it we can get men to check his bike. And I think I'll arrange for Mertoun and Weybridge to come in this afternoon and see if they can spot him.'

The two men went along to the main C.I.D. room. Supervised by two detective constables, seven men were standing in a line, before a row of eight numbered boards placed on the floor.

'Pretty good selection,' congratulated Moss, glancing at the group, who were all dark-haired, but whose height, build and dress were all different. 'Couple like Danny too. Where'd you get them this time?' he asked the policeman.

'Oh, just scrounged around,' smiled one. 'Stood at the front door of the station and grabbed them as they walked past.'

Walking down the line, Thane told them, 'I want to thank you for your co-operation. We won't detain you more than a few minutes. A man is going to join you, then someone will come into the room and look at you all. It is vital, if justice is to be done, that by no word or look you convey any hint to the second man where the first man is standing.'

Shuffling their feet, the seven expressed their understanding.

'Right,' ordered Moss, 'Bring in our man.' One of the detectives departed and returned a moment later with O'Farrell.

'You know the drill, Danny,' said Thane, as the worried looking suspect stared at the line-up. 'Is it a fair parade? And where do you want to stand?'

Gnawing his lip, O'Farrell agreed, 'Seems all right. I'll take number six.' He stood before the placard with the figure "6" on it, and the other seven were shepherded to their places.

'Remember what I said,' warned Thane. 'Right, bring in the witness.'

Wheeler entered the room a moment later, a magazine clutched in one hand.

'I'm not going to mention your name,' Thane told him. 'Just look along this line of men. Take your time. Then, if you see anyone you recognise, just call out the number at his feet, nothing more.'

The mechanic, flushing at being the centre of attention, obeyed. Twice he walked down the line, fairly quickly the first time, more slowly the second, while the eight looked self-consciously ahead. On his second trip, he three times stopped to peer at faces. Then standing back, his voice little more than a whisper, he declared, 'Number six.'

'It's a lie,' shrieked O'Farrell. 'I never saw this character in my life. You're trying to frame me, Thane, you swine.'

He dived across the floor towards the Chief Inspector, fists raised. Moss quickly slid a foot forward, and the safe-blower, arms flailing, tripped and crashed to the boards. The two detective constables had him in a double armlock when he was jerked to his feet.

'That doesn't do you any good,' remarked Thane mildly. He walked over. 'Nice watch you've got there, Danny. Where'd you buy it?'

'From a pal,' whined the safe-blower. 'Look, Mr Thane, for the love of God let me go. I've done nothing.'

'Got a receipt for that watch, Danny?'

'No, what does it matter?' protested O'Farrell.

'Lock him up,' shrugged Thane. 'Make the charge for just now, "being found in possession of property believed stolen without being able to give a satisfactory explanation and being a known thief." That'll do.'

Trembling, unable to struggle in the fierce grip of the two detectives, O'Farrell was led out.

'Sir, I... I...' the mechanic gulped. 'I can't be absolutely certain, you know. It looks awful like him, but there's always the chance I could be wrong.'

'We'll leave that till later,' said Thane. 'Though we'll note what you said.'

He turned to the other seven men, still standing sheepishly in their positions. 'That's all, thanks again. You'll get half-a-crown each to cover any expenses involved. Sorry I can't give you a good horse for this afternoon's races. You might manage to build it up a little if I could.'

Back in his room again, Thane sank wearily into his swivel chair and flipped a cigarette across to Moss. When the two men had lit up, he said in worried tones, 'I don't like it, Phil. I don't like it at all. We're safe enough on that holding charge. The watch is probably stolen, and even if we can't trace it, we can keep him for a day or two, then release him if the murder charge is cleared up.

'But I can't reconcile my mind to Danny in the role of gunman. This Swivney job is far too big for him. We need to keep him on ice, just in case, while we are checking on his story. But the main investigation mustn't let up even a fraction.'

CHAPTER SIXTEEN

UNAWARE OF DANNY O'FARRELL'S sudden, dramatic misfortune, forty men—detectives, plain clothes officers, uniform police—were still hard at work, all with a sense of urgency which overcame the slogging nature of their task.

Every hour that passed meant the trail was growing colder, that the killer might be getting further away, or, if still in the city, was becoming more secure.

Acting on Wheeler's information, they had gone down the short street past the garage and into the main road at the foot. But they could find no one there who had seen the motorcyclist.

Then one young detective had the bright idea of calling at the local Corporation bus depot, and, after some time spent inquiring into timetables, found two drivers who had been passing the corner shortly after the hold-up.

They were in the depot canteen, having a brief break between runs. Driver No. 1 had seen nothing unusual. 'The road's too busy to worry about looking at people,' he said. 'There's enough to do trying not to knock them down.'

But Driver No. 2, a fat, florid individual, hat stuck on the back of his head, did remember a rider.

'He was heading south,' he wheezed to the eager detective. 'No, I can't tell you much about him. He did have a bag, though. I seen him nipping past when we were pulled up at this bus stop. Looked like a young bloke, with his coat collar pulled up, and he had goggles and a beret thing on. It was the bag I noticed. Black, it was, pretty worn too. I wondered what sort of junk he had in it. You know, like the Poles during the war who used to lug briefcases around with nothing but soap and a towel inside.'

The policeman, scribbling shorthand, asked, 'Which way was he heading?'

'South, chum. That road takes you out towards Clarkston way eventually. But I just saw him for a moment, then he nips ahead of a lorry.'

'Notice anything about the bike at all? Do you think you would recognise the man again?'

'Have a heart,' protested the busman. 'I didn't know he was a ruddy murderer. He was just a joker on a bike to me. I just happened to see the bag, that's all, and felt a bit nosy about it.'

The snippet of information was phoned back to Thane. The reference to the "worn black bag" placed it as a possible as distinct from the small mountain of unlikely reports, which alleged that False Face had been in some sixteen widely separate parts of the city within a space of twenty minutes. No description of the leather bag had yet appeared in print, to colour the bus driver's account.

The C.D.I. was grumbling to himself at the reports in the early editions of the evening papers, and having a snack lunch at his desk, when the woman appeared.

Moss brought her in without warning: a young housewife

obviously dressed for the occasion in her best coat and hat. He totally ignored the frown on his chief's face.

'This is Mrs Copelin, sir. Mrs Copelin, this is Chief Detective Inspector Thane, in charge of the case. Will you just tell him what you told the officer who saw you when you came in?'

Thane, with an inward sigh, pushed aside the half-pint milk bottle and closed the packet of sandwiches. He waited until Mrs Copelin was seated, then, offering her a cigarette from his battered packet, said, 'Yes now, what can we do to help?'

The woman declined the offered cigarette. Thane, taking one himself, snapped his lighter to flame as, in a rather embarrassed voice, she began.

'I may be wasting your time, but I felt I'd better tell you...'

Ho, hum, here we go on another amateur detective story, thought Thane as he inhaled the satisfying smoke.

'I think I saw this motorcyclist you are looking for. You know, the one who shot the policeman and stole all that money.'

Thane nodded.

'Well, I was out for a walk with the pram yesterday, in the afternoon. I was turning on my way home to make the tea for Bill—that's my husband, he works in Fairfield's shipyard. Anyway, I was walking along Sittart Street when this motorcycle came along. I noticed it when it turned off the street and went behind the billboards into the waste ground.'

The cigarette burned slowly in Thane's fingers as, suddenly awake, he glanced at Moss.

'Sittart Street, that's about a mile away,' said Moss. In the right direction, too, by the bus driver's story.'

'Go on, Mrs Copelin, tell us anything you can remember,' encouraged Thane.

The woman moistened her lips. 'Well, now, let me see. The man on the motorcycle was carrying something, but I couldn't tell you much more. He was wearing goggles and a beret and an old coat.'

'Did you see his face, Mrs Copelin?' prompted Moss.

'No, I'm afraid I can't help there. You see, the hoardings are on the opposite side of the street from where I was pushing the pram. I just wondered what he was doing at the time, but then I supposed he was parking or something, and just walked on.

'Then I read that you wanted people to help. So, I got my neighbour to look after the baby for an hour and came along.'

'Mrs Copelin, what you have just told us may be important. We'll have to investigate, and we'll do that right now. In the meantime...' Thane lifted his phone. 'Send in Detective Constable Price, please...' Then, replacing the receiver, continued, 'Mr Price will take a proper statement from you. Please don't tell anybody you have been here. I think it's pretty certain the man you saw was this "Mr False Face."'

'Detective Inspector Moss will take a look at this waste ground—oh, and we'll make sure you are run back home by car to that baby of yours.'

Moss was on the telephone within half an hour, a note of satisfaction in his voice.

'Bull's-eye!' he exclaimed. 'No bike or anything like that to be seen, but the ground's pretty soft with the recent rain, and we found some rather interesting marks. I'm no Davy Crockett, but it looks to me as though someone had a car or van there, and maybe took a motorcycle aboard.

'It is difficult to be sure. But there are definite car track marks. Oh, there are other tyre traces all right, here and there. But this particular set have a dent in the ground between them, just where they end, and a light, smaller track, like a motorcycle's, leading to it. I've radioed the scientific department to send down to take casts and that sort of thing.

'There's one other item which might be useful. There was an old bus ticket lying on the ground. It had been run over and pushed into the earth by the car-wheel tracks, just a couple of feet from where they came to a halt. It might have fallen from the car or van, and the wheels might have run over it as the car left.'

'Well worth following it up,' agreed Thane. 'What kind of ticket is it? Oh, a Western company! Tell you what, wait until the scientific people arrive, then head for the Western office. It's in Clyde Street. I'll meet you there in— let's make it forty minutes.'

They met as arranged, and, on entering the bus company office, Thane and Moss were quickly shown into the manager's sanctum, declined cups of tea, accepted cigarettes, then got down to business.

Thane handed the bus official the tiny cellophane envelope, already labelled, signed and sealed, which contained the mud-stained ticket.

'Can you tell us anything about this ticket, sir? Where it was issued, anything like that? I'll have to ask you to leave it inside the envelope. It may be evidence in a case we are investigating.'

The manager raised his eyebrows in surprise, but nodded agreement. 'Excuse me for a few minutes, will you,' he asked. 'I'll take it with me if I may—don't worry, I'll see the envelope stays intact.'

The few minutes were nearer twenty before he returned. 'Sorry about that. But I think I've got some details that may help.' He referred to a slip of paper in his hand.

'The ticket isn't a recent issue. But between the serial number and the cancellation stamps—and, of course by referring to route sheets and the duty rota—that ticket was issued on one of our local services, Southwood suburb to Clyde Street terminus. It is a return, of course, and the second journey was on the same route, from the city out. I can tell you the first journey date, but not the stop at which it was issued. The ticket is twopence short of the full journey fare, you see, and we don't register stops on these tickets. Is that any use to you?'

'Use?' beamed Thane. 'I'll say it is. In fact, it is a lot more than we dreamed. Look, can we ask one more favour. Can you trace the conductress who issued that ticket?'

The busman nodded, but warned, 'It was issued a good many days ago. If you're wondering whether the girl will remember who were passengers on her bus or anything like that, there isn't a hope. Lord knows how many thousand people she has issued tickets to since then.'

Thane pursed his lips. 'You're quite right. I was just getting ahead of myself a little. Never mind just now, sir, and thanks again for your help. I'm sure I can rely on your discretion in the meantime.'

Back in the police car, returning to Millside Station, Thane smiled wryly to himself.

'I wonder, Phil, I wonder. It may have nothing whatever to do with the hold-up. Even if it has a link, it probably won't help us.'

'I'll say it for you,' grunted Moss. 'If it has, you may end up pulling in one of your neighbours, either for helping Danny or, if he wasn't involved, for the actual hold-up. Southwood's pet policeman won't be so popular if he starts grilling the people he travels with on the bus every day.'

Silent, puzzled, Thane mentally agreed as he thought of a "rogues gallery" composed of the morning queues at his local stops.

CHAPTER SEVENTEEN

DAVID RENFIELD HAD BEEN on his way out of the Evening View office, bound for lunch, when the intercom, loudspeakers croaked that he was wanted on the telephone. Picking up the nearest instrument, he had the call—from somewhere outside the office—put through.

'Is that Mr Renfield?' asked the voice. 'Mr Renfield who wrote the front-page story about the big robbery?'

'It is, why?' asked Renfield, puzzled.

'Well, if you've got the time to buy me a drink and if there's some money in it for me, I can give you a red-hot story about it,' said the voice. 'I've just been in a line-up at an identity parade in Millside Police Station.'

'Where can I meet you?' asked Renfield. 'Yes, I know the Friendly Davey pub. All right, I'll meet you in the bar there inside ten minutes.'

Dashing out of the newspaper office, he hailed a passing taxi. It stopped, he climbed aboard, and a few traffic wriggling minutes later, had arrived at his destination. Pushing open the door of the public-house, he walked into the public bar and gazed about.

At the far corner of the bar a middle-aged man in a shabby suit finished his pint of beer, wiped his mouth with his sleeve, and walked across.

'You Renfield? I'm the bloke who phoned. You didn't tell the cops, did you?'

'Newspapers never disclose the source of information,' recited the reporter. 'Now, what have you got to tell me?'

'I've just finished my beer,' said the man significantly. Renfield, beckoning the barman over, ordered two pints of draught beer. As the drinks were placed on the counter and the reporter paid with silver from his pocket, the stranger said, 'I'll sell you my story for five quid. It's worth it.'

'Depends what it is,' countered Renfield. 'If it's a good story the money's yours. Otherwise, you'll have to see what goes into the paper, and we'll pay you what we think it is worth.'

The man hesitated. 'Can I trust that?' he complained.

'Can I trust you?' parried Renfield. 'I haven't got all day. Tell me what this is all about.'

Resolved, the man did.

'I was asked into the police station to take part in this identity parade, see. And the bloke—he was pretty like you, gave me quite a turn when you walked in, it did—was pointed out by this other fellow.

'The bloke who was pointed out went haywire. And do you know what he was wanted for? The murder of that cop. There's a good five quid's worth, mister.'

Renfield whistled and laid his glass down on the countertop. 'This witness—was he a man in overalls, a mechanic?' he asked.

His companion nodded.

'Thanks a lot. I'll have to fly. Buy another one on me.' He planked a half-crown on the bar counter and made to leave.

'Here, what about my fiver?' protested the man.

'Call at the office later this afternoon,' called Renfield over his shoulder, then was gone.

He caught a tram back along Argyle Street, and sat on the top deck, puzzling over this latest development.

"If he's right, Thane has nailed someone for the murder," he told himself, in a mixture of triumph and bewilderment.

Not for a moment did any sympathy for the unknown prisoner enter his head. In the long hours that had passed since he had fired the three shots from the automatic a complete mental change of outlook had come over the reporter. Self-preservation and personal gain were now the only two motives remaining in his money-warped mind.

"If the police have pulled in someone. I'm in the clear," he told himself. "I'll be sitting pretty, with some poor sucker having to carry the can."

He jumped off the tram as it neared the View office, positively sprinted up the stairs to the editorial, and got on the phone to Millside Police.

'Mr Thane is not in just now,' said a voice when he finally got through to the C.I.D. room. 'Sergeant MacLean here. Can I help you?'

'Hello Mac, it's David Renfield of the View here. When will the boss be back?'

'Don't know, David. He's out with Inspector Moss somewhere and didn't leave any message behind.'

'Maybe you can help me, Mac. We've had word that you have got someone in for the payroll murder. Is it true?'

There was a pregnant silence on the line. Then MacLean declared, 'You'll have to ask the boss that one, David. No comment from this cog in the machine.'

'Thanks, Mac, you didn't say a thing,' grinned Renfield, replacing the telephone. He turned to his typewriter, flipped a sheet of paper into it, and his fingers raced over the keys.

VIEW EXCLUSIVE

Glasgow police are understood to have questioned a man in connection with the murder of Police Constable Ewan Macrae and the theft of the Swivney factory payroll.

The man has been detained at Millside Police Station for further questioning.

He pulled the sheet out of the machine. 'Boy,' he yelled, and as a copy-boy appeared at his elbow, 'Take this to the subs' desk... tell the copy-taster there's more coming.'

CHAPTER EIGHTEEN

THREE MESSAGES WERE LYING on Colin Thane's desk when he returned to the police station from his visit to the bus company office.

Message No. 1 was to the effect that both the Swivney cashier and chauffeur would be along at 4 p.m. and, as he had directed, an identity parade would be arranged for that time.

Message No. 2 was that Renfield of the View had telephoned and would call back.

The third, and final, note brought a frown to his face. It was a report from the Scientific Branch, who had made a quick examination of Danny O'Farrell's motorcycle in a garage near his tenement home.

"The machine is definitely not the one used in the payroll robbery. Its basic colour is blue, the original paint in which the bike was finished. Tyre patterns are different from those traces discovered at the murder locus."

He glanced at the clock on the wall. 3.15 p.m. Three-quarters of an hour before the two Swivney men were due. Thane sighed, swung his leg over the arm of his swivel chair into his familiar, comfortable position, and took the first bundle of paperwork out of the wire mesh basket on his desk.

The top sheet was a teleprinter request from Birmingham C.I.D. for a man to meet two of their officers travelling north by train that night and due in Glasgow the next morning. They were coming to pick up the wanted man who had been accidentally dredged up in the overnight police search.

Scrawling "Meet with car" and his initials at the foot of the page, he picked up the next item, and groaned. His heart wasn't in such matters as the monthly statistical return of crime in his division. He tried again. Worse. It was the duty rota for the next month's shift work.

Putting down the papers, he let his mind wander over the facts which had so far accumulated in the case.

A medium-build man with dark hair had robbed the car and shot Macrae. A medium-build man with dark hair, who had raced away from the area with a bag over his arm, had been identified by the mechanic as Danny O'Farrell. Danny owned a motorbike. But Danny's bike was definitely not the machine which had been used in the operation.

No weapon had yet been found—and Danny had never been known to use anything but his fists.

The bike seemed to have been lifted into a van at the waste ground and smuggled away. If the bus ticket was a connecting link, did this mean that someone from Southwood was helping the Gorbals safe-blower?

Danny? Had it been Danny? Wheeler had been nearly positive in his identification, too positive to let a possible armed murderer run loose again.

"If there was a gang behind all this, Danny might have gathered the necessary gumption to carry out the principal role, especially if someone else was giving the orders and doing the organizing," mused Thane.

"He had the time to do it after he left the Labour Exchange. He might have deliberately kicked up that fuss to impress himself on the clerk's memory. And all he can say about after he left the Exchange is that he went window shopping.

"And why would Wheeler, who'd never seen O'Farrell before, pick him out as not only a motorcyclist, but the motorcyclist who had scorched past the garage?"

Thane was still gazing blankly across the room, his mind puzzling over the situation, when there was a knock at the door, and an orderly announced that Mertoun and Weybridge, the Swivney cashier and chauffeur, had arrived. They were with Moss, who was ready to commence the second identity parade.

The parade lasted fifteen minutes. First the cashier, then the chauffeur inspected the line of eight men.

There was a fresh selection of dark-haired "suspects" into which Danny O'Farrell had once more been slipped. This time Danny had chosen number seven spot. It was a luckier choice than his earlier number. Neither the cashier nor the chauffeur could select anyone from the line.

'The man had this mask on over his face all the time,' said Mertoun. 'But I seem to remember him having well-trimmed, fairly short hair. No, there's no one here I can place.'

Danny had murmured a little prayer of thanksgiving for his long thick locks—but had still been bundled back to his cell.

Frustration and indecision mounting within him, Thane returned to his room. He was just about to peck once more at the contents of the wire basket when the telephone rang a rescuing peal.

'This is Jock Mills of the Evening Hour, Mr Thane. What's the strength of this story the View are running about you having questioned a suspect in connection with the murder?'

'What!' With an angry, bear-like growl, Thane, glaring at the receiver, demanded, 'What do they say?'

Mills read the View's splash story over to the detective.

'It is in their second last edition,' he explained. 'Is it true? We might manage to squeeze something in our last run... the boss is feeling peeved at me for missing it.'

'We have nothing, absolutely nothing, to say at this stage,' barked Thane. 'No one has been charged, and our inquiries are continuing. Now get off the line. I want to find out what the hell's going on!'

He rapped the receiver rest up and down until the switchboard operator answered.

'Get me the View office right away,' he ordered. 'I want to speak to a reporter called Renfield.' The mysterious buzzes, clicks and rattles that are part of every switchboard operator's stock-in-trade lasted only a few seconds. Then Renfield's voice came over the wires, cautious in tone.

'Hello, Mr Thane. Renfield here.'

'What do you think you and that rag of a paper of yours are playing at with this story about a man being questioned?' demanded Thane, in angry tones so loud that, at the other end of the wire, the reporter hurriedly held the phone away from his ear.

'Where did you get your information?' persisted Thane.

'We never divulge that sort of thing, Chief Inspector, you know that,' protested Renfield. 'It's true, isn't it?'

'True be damned. Look, young fellow. You helped me this morning. I gave you a story and some off-the-record advice. Now I'm going to tell you something. No one has been charged with murder yet. Until anyone is, this sort of story is a direct interference with our work. I want to see no more of these wild stories. If there are, you have had your last interview out of me.'

He banged down the phone, still smouldering. Gradually, however, he returned to a more reasonable frame of mind, and finally a hint of a smile tugged at the corners of his mouth.

"I don't know." He shook his head. "Sometimes I think these ruddy newspapers have reporters hidden in every wastepaper basket. We could do with a few fact finders like Renfield and company in the C.I.D. right now."

He turned back to the work on his desk.

CHAPTER NINETEEN

THE CANTEEN TROLLEY was wending its tea-and-wad way around the editorial flat in the Evening View office. In the partitioned-off section that was the reporters' room the day's bustle had temporarily died, the rattle of typewriters had fallen to an occasional clack.

The main edition had gone, routine anti-climax was setting in.

Wandering over from the sub-editors' desk, Jimmy Dodds had started off by talking about the prospects for the following day's football programme, and the football pool coupon which he had just posted, and then drifted round to the day's splash story.

George Kendal, one of the younger reporters, just in from covering a road smash, chipped into the talk as he hung his rain-soaked coat on the rack.

'This character who shot the policeman is probably a nut,' he declared, lighting a flamboyantly carved pipe he pulled from his pocket. 'A real nut. And when they do catch him, they'll parade about three doctors who'll say he was frightened by a postman at the age of two and goes away with the fairies whenever he sees a uniform.

'He'll end up in a nice comfy loony bin for a few years, living on the fat of the land... then come out and start doing in people all over again.'

Cries of protest from the others in the group failed to deter him.

'No man in his right mind goes shooting other people in cold blood,' he protested.

'That sort of thing happens in America, maybe even in London now and then. But they're both full of trigger-happy types. No home-brewed thug is going to start that sort of thing —unless he's a nut.'

'That's stupid, George,' said Dodds. 'There are plenty of men—especially men who went through the tougher side of the war—who would kill without a qualm. And what about the man who panics? This business of a man with a gun panicking in a tight spot is an old, old story. There have been plenty of armed hold-ups in Scotland before, you know. It just happens that people seldom get killed. Look, David, you're on the story. What do the police think about this chappy they've got hold of?'

Renfield, who had been sitting quietly, outwardly disinterested, looked up, struggling to restrain the flush he felt stealing over his face.

'I don't know what the police think about him... I don't even know who he is. Probably the police don't particularly care at this stage what his reasons were. But, though he deserves all he gets, this poor devil must be going through hell.'

'Aye, right,' laughed Kendal. 'You can buy a lot of fireproof clothing with the money he got.'

Renfield's mouth tightened. 'For God's sake, George, stop thinking in terms of "B" feature films.

'This man's killed. You don't know why he killed, the fear that must have gripped him, the terror he feels now every time he crosses a road, the waiting for a knock at his door, a hand on his shoulder.

'You don't know how desperately he needed the money. Haven't you ever done anything in your miserable little life that was almost a reflex action, then felt like crying the next minute, felt you'd give anything just to live that time over again and change things, but knew that you couldn't, and that you just had to go on and say to hell with anyone who got in your way...

His voice died away, he turned from the group. Behind his back eyebrows were raised, and a protesting Kendal asked, 'What's bitten old David? What sent him off the handle like that?'

A shout from the news editor's room brought relief to the depression that had suddenly seized the young reporter. He walked over to the glass-fronted office and was waved into a seat—a rare honour, reserved for occasions when a man was either to be praised or sacked.

This afternoon was to be a praise session. McRowder made this clear by offering him a peppermint from the little bag he always carried.

'Grand piece of work you did today, David. Editor's pleased as punch, and we've made the Hour look like a sick cat. Even the Advertising Manager's getting someone to spell the words out to him, and when that illiterate son realises there's something other than his precious comic strips it's a really good story. I'm putting you through for a bonus, and if you keep on like this on the story, well, there may be a nice rise in your pay packet.'

Renfield murmured his thanks. 'What do you want me to do?' he asked.

'Just keep on as you're doing. Treat it your own way. The way I see it, even if the police have got someone, there will be a day or two before they finally charge him. Then there's the court appearance, some inquiries about what the other big firms are doing in the way of extra precautions, all sorts of things. The story can run big for the best part of next week.

'Oh, and the Editor's got a good idea. He wants you to get hold of a false-face mask from some shop or other to act as a sort of trade mark for the following days' stories.'

The interview was over. McRowder switched off his smile and resumed his normal deadpan expression. Renfield went back to his desk, feeling as pleased as a dog with two tails.

Everything was going his way. Everything... and that included Jean.

They weren't due to meet that night, but suddenly he felt he needed her company, wanted her to be caught up in the thrill of excitement which was gathering inside him.

It took a little time to get Miss Catta to the telephone in Madame Valdesco's dress salon. There was a slight edge to her voice when she finally answered. Madame V.—nee Mr Isadore Rabinski—had been holding a fashion show that afternoon. And Jean had had an extremely trying time, as had the other mannequins, in coping with Mr Rabinski's raging temperament.

But her tone changed at Renfield's opening gambit of a trip through to Edinburgh, dinner, then on to a show. And when, two hours later, he drew his Ford into the pavement's edge outside the dress shop, she was waiting to greet him.

They drove out of town, along Alexandra Parade, and onto the long, straight main Edinburgh road. Glancing at the petrol gauge, which was flickering around the quarter-full mark, Renfield decided to stop at the first filling station.

It was only when the first four of the six gallons of petrol he had ordered had been pumped into the tank that he suddenly remembered that in the day's hustle and anxiety, he had forgotten to pick up his pay packet. He glanced at Jean, smiling by his side. 'Damn,' he declared, 'I've left my pay in the office.'

Her smile clouded. Making up his mind, he forced a chuckle into his voice. 'All right, though, Uncle David's got a little left.'

The wad of money he had taken from the stolen bag was still in his pocket. Thane had told him that morning that the police couldn't trace the one-pound notes. Pulling the bundle from his pocket, he stripped two notes from it and handed them out of the window to the attendant. Jean's eyes widened perceptibly.

'Well,' she murmured. 'We look like painting the town red on that.'

Spending the first of his haul, even on a mundane purchase like petrol, seemed to release a last lock inside the reporter.

'A warm blush pink,' he corrected. 'We'll do the best we can, anyway.' Waving away the silver change the pump attendant was bringing over, he slid the Ford into first gear, let the clutch pedal out—and promptly stalled the engine. He had forgotten to let the handbrake off.

That "warm blush pink" stole over his face. But Jean only laughed and slid possessively nearer.

The car went roaring on its way.

They had dinner in a hot, noisy, but highly fashionable restaurant off Princes Street, complete with a bottle of wine. The walls and ceilings were gay with decorations for Hallowe'en night. Witches rode broomsticks across the menu. Imitation turnip lanterns burned on every table.

Afterwards, they walked the short distance to the theatre, arm in arm, laughing and joking as they passed groups of children dressed in an assortment of strange and fanciful home-made costumes, disguised behind both fierce and friendly masks.

Then he saw the child. A boy, not more than ten, a sheet wrapped around him as a cloak, a battered soft hat, probably borrowed from his father, on his head. Like the others he was wearing a "false face."

It was a flesh-coloured mask with a bright red nose... it was the duplicate of the one he had worn in the hold-up...

Renfield's grip tightened on Jean's arm, his voice wavered. She began a surprised protest.

But the sudden, punch-like shock had passed. He let go of her arm, slid his arm round her waist instead. The incident passed amid her giggled protest and Jean's gentle but firm return of his hand to her arm.

After the show, they had supper in a quiet little place which specialised in soft lights and softer music, knees touching beneath the tiny table. The wad of notes had considerably shrunk when, a slight but buoyant swagger in his walk, he escorted Jean back to the car and they set off on their return journey back to Glasgow.

Inevitably, they stopped in one of the many little lay-bys on the road, designed to allow lorries to halt while their drivers rested, but at night island havens for motorised courting. Nuzzling her ear, feeling the soft, firm contours of her body pressing against his, David Renfield whispered words which he had been scared to utter until then; words which tightened Jean's arms around him.

Finally, agonizingly slowly, he told her, 'Jean, I need you. Say you'll marry me.'

He felt her body tense. They sat silent for a moment. Then, in a strained voice, she replied, 'Darling, I'm very fond, very, very fond of you. But don't ask me just yet. I've told you before that I've got ambitions, that I want things out of life.'

'You've told me,' agreed Renfield. 'And Jean, the only reason I've had the courage to ask you is because things have changed with me. I've won money, a lot of money. Enough to let us do most of the things we both want. Between that and my job, and the rise I've been promised, we could be on Easy Street.

'I haven't told anybody else about my luck. It's a secret between you and I. Think about it, Jean; think about it really hard. And let me know as quickly as you can.'

They drove on shortly after that. They kissed once more in the car, faces lit by a faint glow from the instrument panel light. Then she disappeared into the tenement close, and he heard her high heels tapping up the stairs.

When he drove the car into the lock-up garage a little later, Renfield sat for a while, the silence only disturbed by faint noises from the cooling engine and exhaust.

Should he have told Jean so soon, he wondered? Still, the damage was done, and there was little likelihood of her ever guessing the shape his "luck" had taken.

Stepping out, he flicked his cigarette lighter to life and by its wavering light examined the motorcycle lying against the wall.

The marks of the fall were there, only slight scrapes it was true. But they might be noticed by its owner, John Dawkins, when he came in tomorrow—no, it was today now, it was after midnight. John usually took the machine out about nine o'clock on a Saturday morning, to use it over the weekend before returning it once more to rest in the lock-up during the working week.

He was a careless devil when it came to the appearance of the machine, but he might notice the scratches and, slow on the uptake though he was, he might remember the newspaper stories of the masked killer and put two and two together.

Renfield pursed his lips. There was a simple way out of the problem, a way almost sure to work. His light-hearted mood was fully restored as he crept into the house to avoid waking his landlady. He paused only to wind the alarm clock at his bedside before he prepared for sleep.

CHAPTER TWENTY

BY THE TIME Thane decided it was time to take a break from work and go home for a meal the work of gathering statements, collecting information and filing reports had considerably progressed at the murder hunt base in Millside Police Station.

A haggard-faced Danny O'Farrell was still protesting his innocence to everyone who came within earshot of his quarters in the cell block.

Three bullets, one from each of the Rolls' punctured tyres, one from the heart of the young constable, now lay on the Chief Inspector's desk, each in its sealed and labelled envelope. Beside them lay the bus ticket, a faint and far-fetched clue which had brought the case into a strange new perspective within the last half-hour.

A telephone call from the bus depot manager had confirmed the previous information given regarding the ticket.

'We've been examining the conductresses' waybills again,' he had added. 'From them, we can tell the run that any ticket was issued on. That ticket was on the 8.23 a.m. bus from

Southwood. I'm sorry we can't say what time of day the return half was used, the girls only cancel the second portion.'

The 8.23 a.m. was Thane's regular bus. He gazed at the little oblong of paper while the faces of his fellow passengers, some friendly and frank, others sour and sleepy, floated through his mind.

When he finally left the police station, Thane found a C.I.D. car waiting at the main door. But, instead, he followed his usual practice and walked down to the Clyde Street terminus. Boarding the Southwood bus, he sat in the back seat on the upper deck, eyes flickering over the packed ranks of office workers before him.

Was one a thief and a murderer?

He dismissed killers and payrolls, tickets and tragedy from his mind as he swung open the garden gate of his home. The front door of the house was unlocked as he walked up the path, a shaft of light shot out from the hallway, and he was rushed upon by his two shouting children, their mongrel dog yelping eagerly in the background.

A hug for Kate, who was lugging a bedraggled doll in one hand, a ruffle of the hair for his son Tom, and he stepped into the hallway.

His wife was waiting. They kissed, an affectionate peck, and he sighed in relief. 'Good to be home, Mary dear. Only time for a meal and a change of clothes, though. I'll need to go in for a while again this evening. I'll try and be back for supper if all goes well.'

Mrs Thane, long since resigned to the difficulties of being a policeman's wife, smiled as they entered the living room, where the table had been set.

'The kids have been dooking for apples,' she told him. 'I promised you'd have a try. Oh, and Colin, I know the horrible connection Hallowe'en masks have with this murder, but you won't mind, will you, if they wear the ones you brought them?'

'Mind? Of course not—now give me a fork and lead me to that tub,' chuckled Thane gleefully.

A certain Detective Inspector would have laughed till he burst if, during the next few minutes, he had seen the look of tremendous concentration on his superior's face. Spurred on by whoops from a Red Indian and a Green-Eyed Martian, Colin Thane grimly set about the task of dropping a fork from between his teeth onto the target presented by a dozen large red apples bobbing about in what, many years ago, had been a baby's bathtub.

Then came the meal. And after it, while the children were gobbling nuts in front of the fireplace, he smoked a couple of cigarettes, glanced through the selection of bills that had come with the morning post, and finally retired to soak in the luxury of a hot bath.

Just over two hours after he had arrived home, he phoned for a car to pick him up. Half an hour later he was back at his desk.

Moss had no development to report. 'The mills are grinding, but slow,' he grunted. 'Things are so quiet I even managed to get out for a decent meal.'

Crunching one of his Vitamin C tablets between his teeth — 'just to keep my juices balanced'—he went on, 'Oh, we had an offer of professional services. A crank diviner who says he can locate guns under water with a hazel twig. He wants to float down the Clyde in a boat looking for our murder weapon.'

Thane grinned. 'It's queer the types of people who come flocking round whenever sudden death breaks loose. All we want is the usual fake confession by someone whose wife doesn't understand him and feels that prison would be a happier place than home, and we'll be in standard pattern.

'Talking of fake confessions, I'm going to give the press boys a line tonight. It'll take their minds off the View story of a suspect being questioned—I don't want any further word of Danny getting out. You know these anonymous letters we always get... "Mrs A's been spending money, where's she getting it all" sort of thing? Well, I'll tell the lads we've had one suggesting the possible killer. There actually were two screwball letters like that in the afternoon mail, though there was nothing to them.'

A pained look crossed Moss's face.

'Oh, it's all right,' said Thane. 'It will keep the story alive and public interest awake, which is what we want as much as the newspapers at this stage. And it may give Mr False Face a few anxious hours, if, as I've an awfully strong feeling, he isn't our friend Danny.'

"Friend Danny" had his fate finally sealed in dramatic fashion about an hour later, when a Central Division car brought a middle-aged uniform constable from that area over to the Millside Station to see Thane.

'Constable Jackman, sir,' he introduced himself. 'I changed over shifts today and only came on duty about tea-time. Don't think me impertinent, sir, but I heard from my neighbour that you've got Danny O'Farrell in here. The buzz is that you're holding him in connection with yesterday's shooting. Is that right, sir?'

'Since you've obviously got a good reason for asking, the answer is yes. There's no charge made yet, though. We're holding him for something else. Why?'

The constable shifted uncomfortably. 'Well, I felt I had to come and tell you, sir. He couldn't have done the shooting. It would have been impossible.'

'Go on, man,' encouraged Thane. 'Don't worry about

hurting either my feelings or my case. I personally don't think Danny's got either the guts or the brains for it.'

'This shooting was about three in the afternoon, wasn't it, sir? At three o'clock I was on duty in Argyle Street, on the north footway. And I saw Danny O'Farrell there. I'd know him anywhere. Twice I've arrested him, and once we had a whale of a fight on a Saturday night before I knocked sufficient sense into his head to get him to come quietly.

'Knowing his record, I kept an eye on him for a bit. He just wandered along, though I noticed that he seemed to be paying a lot of attention to a cafe at one place... you may know the one, sir, it's just next door to a pub. It would be nearly fifteen minutes later before he moved away. So, you see, sir, I know it just couldn't have been Danny.'

With an exasperated laugh, Thane sank back in his chair. 'I might have known it. Just a moment, Constable.' He rose, left his room, and returned with Moss.

'This is Inspector Moss, Constable. Just repeat your story again, will you?'

The policeman did so. As he concluded, the two detectives looked at one another with mixed emotions.

'Remember the plan you found, Phil?' asked Thane. 'Will you take a bet that Danny was out spying the land for his next safe-blowing? Lucky for him that Jackman saw him.'

'What do we do with him now?'

'Put the fear of death into him and kick him out,' declared Thane. 'I'll come and help you.'

Down in the cell block, quiet and still awaiting the usual rush of Friday night customers after pub-closing, O'Farrell was sitting on his bunk, head cupped in his hands.

'All right, Danny, come out. Your worries are over,' said Moss, as the turnkey unlocked the iron-barred door. 'You're a lucky son, you are. A policeman remembers seeing you.'

'That's right, Danny,' added Thane, as the safe-blower, disbelief written over his face, stood up in the cell. 'We're going to drop that charge about the watch. Don't be too clever though. We could probably make it stick. Then there's the little matter of that plan we found at your home, and the fact that the cafe you were seen outside looks awfully like the one in the drawing.

'We're letting you go, Danny. But maybe you've had a big enough fright to make you go straight.'

'Don't I get any compensation?' whined O'Farrell, as he began to realise that he really was being allowed free. 'You've had me locked up all day, you've accused me of murdering a bloke. I'm entitled to compensation.'

'You'll be entitled to my boot in a tender place,' declared Moss. 'You heard what Mr Thane said. We can have you put away for a nice little stretch, but we're letting you go because we've got big hearts. Now get moving, and keep your mouth shut. And if as much as a bottle of beer goes missing from that pub I'll come after you and blow you up with one of your own detonators!'

CHAPTER TWENTY-ONE

GLOOM WAS WRITTEN large over Moss's face when he returned from watching O'Farrell retrieve his personal belongings, taken from him when he was searched on arrest and kept in the police office safe. 'We seem to be right back at the beginning again,' he declared to Thane.

'Not quite,' corrected the Chief Inspector. 'We have prevented a safe-blowing, wiped a suspect off our list, and we know one, possibly two, things more about the man we're hunting.

'First, he has got a neatly cut head of hair. Mertoun's memory was jogged on that point by the parade. And a possible second, we have the bus ticket. You didn't laugh when I said I had a hunch that Danny was telling the truth. Well, I've got another hunch. It is that that bus ticket holds the solution to the whole mystery.'

Cautiously, Moss reminded him, 'It could have been blown there.'

'It could have. But I think it was dropped by accident by

Mr False Face. And that mark you found was almost definitely where the motorcycle was lifted into some kind of van. The Scientific Branch say that the tyre marks on the vacant ground are identical with the marks they found in the lane.

'Part of our problem now is whether this was a one-man job, or whether someone else helped False Face in his getaway.

'Right now, however, I think we should take a run round to see young Wheeler, the mechanic. Do you have his address handy? I think he lives out Springburn way.'

Nodding, Moss pulled his notebook from one pocket and rapidly flicked over the pages. 'Here we are, 14 Balluderon Street, Springburn,' he announced. 'If we want to catch him in, though, it's a bad night. Friday night is when he probably takes his girl out, or goes round to the local for a drink with his pals.'

'My little ray of sunshine. Really, Phil,' grinned Thane, 'I don't know what I'd do without your constant encouragement. Shove your coat on and get your biscuits. We'll go and pay a call on Mr Wheeler.'

They were in luck. Jimmy Wheeler, on his return to the garage in the early afternoon, had discovered his boss pacing frantically up and down, and had immediately been told that if he was finished playing at blue-pencil detectives there was work to be done.

'This lorry had come in with two broken springs,' he explained. 'I didn't get finished that job until about half-past seven, and by the time I got home and had something to eat it wasn't worthwhile going out. So, I've just been sitting here listening to Radio Luxembourg. They've some grand jazz programmes on a Friday.'

'We want to ask you a few more questions, Jimmy,' Thane told the mechanic. 'You see, the man you picked out at the identity parade has had to be released. He had a cast-iron alibi for the time of the murder. I'm not trying to be funny at your expense, son. But tell me, how good is your eyesight?'

The mechanic, face going as red as the check in the tartan sports shirt which, with blue jeans, white socks and leather "casuals" was his garb for this evening at home, flushed indignantly.

'My eyes are fine. I told you there was always the chance I was wrong, though I'd almost swear he was the man. In fact, if it wasn't him, it must have been his twin brother.'

'Could it have been somebody pretty like him?' helped Thane.

'Well... you see this bloke just whizzed past the garage. It was the way he was riding I noticed. I didn't bother about his face until the next morning when that reporter asked me. Och, maybe it was somebody else. But it was somebody who looked pretty like him, all right.'

'There's nothing much more we can ask you for now, Jimmy. We'll be getting in touch with you later,' said Thane, rising to leave.

Thane and Moss arrived back at Millside just as the first cars bringing reporters along for the late-night press conference were pulling up outside the police station.

The next fifteen minutes were tricky ones, as Thane fenced off the barrage of questions concerning the View story that a man had been held for questioning.

'We did question a man concerning his movements,' he admitted. 'But there was a completely satisfactory explanation to our inquiries, and there was no question of the man being held on any charge connected with the murder.

'There's no sense in following up that line. Here's a tit-bit for you, though.'

Face straight, he told them of the "letter" he had received.

'Are you acting on the information in it?' pressed one reporter eagerly.

'We are making inquiries into it, as we would into any such letter,' replied Thane.

CHAPTER TWENTY-TWO

"ANONYMOUS LETTER MURDER MAN," screamed the morning papers. "Police Pounce Imminent," yelled slightly smaller type.

If Colin Thane could have seen Renfield's reaction to the headlines, and known his connection with the case, he would have been satisfied.

The reporter, dressed in a favourite brown tweed suit, had swung downstairs shortly before 8 a.m. The morning paper was waiting beside his breakfast table, and the regular Saturday menu of bacon and eggs, toast and coffee was being brought in by his landlady just as he unfolded the tabloid.

Her greeting passed unheard as he stared at the heavy black type, his first reaction one of panic. But he continued reading, paper held rigidly before him.

'Good morning,' repeated the landlady. Then, 'Is there something wrong... are you not feeling well?'

'No, no, sorry, I was just so busy reading. It was rude of me,' he told her.

'All this hard work and staying out late isn't good for you,

you know?' Mrs Senior scolded in worried tones. 'You'll end up in bed, sick, at this rate.'

'I feel all right, really, Mrs Senior,' he reassured her once more.

She left the room, shaking her head, repeating, 'You'll end up in bed, sick.'

As the door closed, leaving him alone in the room, Renfield, food untouched before him, read the story once more and wondered just how much there was behind it. This sort of trick had been pulled before in murder cases.

"Psychological warfare," was the phrase Thane had used to describe it when, being run into town one morning, he had revealed how an English police chief had once scared a suspect out into the open by announcing similar tidings. There was only a thin chance that the letter was genuine, an even thinner chance that it named him.

"If it was thought at all genuine, Thane would have kept his mouth tight shut," he told himself. "It's meant to scare, nothing more. It must be."

But if it was meant to scare, who was its target? He could think of no way any suspicion could have fallen on him. Surely the garage mechanic hadn't tumbled to his colossal mistake. Or had Thane lied when he said that the one-pound notes couldn't be traced?

He cursed his stupidity in spending the money in Edinburgh the night before. But, steadying his thoughts, he decided, "They can't know the numbers. If they did, and if Thane had traced them, I'd have been picked up before now."

But the worry remained. Mrs Senior found an uneaten breakfast and her lodger gone when she returned half an hour later. And before Renfield left the house, he unlocked the suitcase in his room, and put the automatic which had lain in it into his pocket.

The hands of his wristwatch were just leaving eight-thirty when Renfield reached the lock-up garage. John Dawkins, the motorcyclist, should arrive about nine, ready to take his machine out.

Waiting for him would make Renfield late for work. But the next half-hour might prove vital in covering up his tracks. If all went well, what he planned to do would be the flourish which would sign the end of possible pursuit.

Cautiously, ears pricked for the sound of the other man's approach, he wheeled the motorcycle round inside the Nissen until the side which had been scratched when he skidded it to the ground was nearest the corrugated iron wall, not far from the door. One hand on the handlebar, the other resting on the pillion seat, he waited, stamping his feet and shivering in the chill of the morning.

The sound of cheerful whistling announced Dawkins' approach just a few minutes after nine. Hidden by the angle of the lock-up's walls, Renfield waited until he judged the man to be only a few yards away.

Then, deliberately, he pushed the bike forward and away from him, and let go. It slid down the wall with a harsh grating of metal on metal, and as it did, he shouted in as anxious tones as he could muster.

Dawkins' feet thudded the last few yards. When the young owner of the motorcycle looked in the entrance, he found a seemingly crestfallen driver bending to pick up the machine.

'What on earth—oh, it's you, David. Here, what's happened to my ruddy bike?' he asked.

Renfield, leaving the *Dot* lying, turned, a look of surprise and distress on his face. 'Sorry, John,' he replied smoothly. 'I was just moving the bike out of the road for a minute while I got the car clear, and I lost my balance. Here, I'll pick it up. I hope there's nothing wrong.'

He raised the machine before its owner could say anything more. There were fresh scratches added to those he had made two days before. 'It's got scraped a bit,' he apologised. 'Don't worry though, I'll get it fixed.'

The motorcyclist bent over the machine and gave the marks a cursory glance.

'You're a careless clown. Och, don't worry, it isn't anything that matters. The *Dot's* had plenty of paint scraped off it in its time. Buy me a tin of cellulose, and we'll call it square,' he grinned.

There was nothing fake about the look of relief which swept across the reporter's face. John Dawkins had swallowed the "accident" idea, hook, line and sinker.

'Well, I'm glad to hear that,' he brightened. Then, unable to resist capping his performance, 'You'd better watch, though. The police over in Millside are looking for a man with a motor-cycle that looks scraped about a bit. They still haven't caught that "Mr False Face" character.'

Dawkins, a small, slim young man with a shock of red hair, roared with laughter.

'They'd have a job to pin that one on me,' he chortled. 'Here, do you know what happened to me on Thursday? Well, the firm are on the brink of a big sales push—advertising, competitions, free gifts, the lot. And the boss threw a boozy lunch for some of the out-of-town sales managers on Thursday. I was kept running around like a ruddy footman. They were all half canned by the time it was over. They'll surely remember the wee fellow that helped them back to the office in time to get organised and away home. At least two of them swore their undying friendship to me!'

He howled with mirth at the recollection. 'No, I'd have little bother proving where I got to that afternoon.'

'What are you going to be doing this weekend?' asked Renfield. 'Are you going away at all?'

'As a matter of fact, yes. I'm going away climbing this weekend. I'll stay overnight at a youth hostel and come back on Sunday night. There were to have been two other chaps coming with me, actually, but they've had to call off.

'David, I don't suppose you'd like to come along and have a try at it? It's great fun.'

Renfield hurriedly cut him short. 'Some people have to work, I'm afraid. Still, thanks for the offer—and my apologies once more about the bike. I'll need to get weaving now. There was a little bit of bother with the car this morning, nothing serious, just a loose wire. But I'm late. Be seeing you.'

He got into the shooting brake, pulled the choke, and pressed the starter button. The engine roared to life, and he began to reverse out of the lock-up, with a farewell wave through the window to the young man, who was busily engaged in booting the kick-start of his bike.

It took speedy, forceful driving to get to the Millside Police Station in time for the 10 a.m. conference which had been arranged.

The old gang of pressmen were there, joined by some Sunday paper types, and the latter, new to the case, had already been firing questions at Detective Inspector Moss, who was standing in for his chief.

'Where's old Thane?' chirruped one newsman.

'Chief Detective Inspector Thane, to you, my friend, is over with the Chief Constable at the moment,' replied Moss with heavy humour.

'Does that mean the Chief's worried?' demanded another.

But Moss, no newcomer to the rough-and-tumble style of interview, blocked the thrust with an irritatingly formal, 'A routine report on the progress of investigations is being made.'

Then someone asked the question Renfield hadn't dared to put.

'What about the anonymous letter?'

Moss ran a finger around his collar edge, allowing a slight grin to slide across his angular face. 'Well, of course, we always get anonymous letters,' he admitted. 'Let's say nothing more about that and think that it made a good story.'

A chorus of groans came from the assembled pressmen.

'Really, I'm sorry, boys. There's nothing fresh yet. But I've got things to do. Away and write your usual lies,' he dismissed them.

Renfield hung back as the rest of the group reluctantly left the office and stood quietly, looking at the detective inspector.

'Well, David,' smiled Moss. 'I hear Colin Thane fairly gave you a chewing on the phone yesterday afternoon.'

'He certainly did,' agreed the reporter. 'But I was right, wasn't I? You did have someone in, and, even if you didn't charge him, you came pretty close to it?'

'It can do no harm now, so I'll tell you—strictly off the record, of course—what it was that happened. We did pull in someone, a South Side ned who not only is on our books as a motorcyclist but was picked out by that mechanic you found as the man he had seen. And we were just about ready to throw the book at him when his alibi turned up—in the shape of a Central Division cop who'd spent about a quarter of an hour watching him at the time when we thought he had been pulling the hold-up.

'So, we had to let him go... and he scurried away quickly enough, I'll tell you.'

'The tip-off was genuine, then,' smiled Renfield. 'How did the mistake come about?'

'Don't know. Young Wheeler says he was sure at the time that it was this ned we picked up. But now he agrees he didn't pay too much attention to the man on the bike. I don't blame him for his mistake. Remembering faces is bad enough when it only involves people you're supposed to know. Trying to recall a face you only glimpsed for a few seconds, a face you weren't particularly interested in, is a difficult matter. If it wasn't, a good few men walking around free as air would be stacked inside our prisons.'

Renfield mustered enthusiasm into his words of agreement, and asked, 'Incidentally, I don't suppose any of the money has turned up? Mr Thane mentioned you knew the numbers of the ten-shilling notes, though, of course, that wasn't for publication.'

'Situation's still the same. The ten-bob notes are the only chances we have,' confirmed Moss.

'Thanks. Well, I'll need to start back for the office,' said the reporter. 'I'm going to contact one or two banks and some of the bigger firms and see if they are contemplating any changes in their security arrangements. There might be quite a good little story to be worked up there.'

As Renfield left, Moss turned on his heel back into his little room. Opening a drawer of his desk, he took out the bottle of olive oil, and regarded it with something akin to distaste.

'I don't know which is worse,' he muttered. 'Putting up with my aches and pains, or having to swallow this stuff.'

He took out a tablespoon, and poured a dose. The taste of the oil was still lingering in his mouth when he heard Thane returning from his visit to Police Headquarters.

'How'd it go,' queried Moss. 'The boss upset?'

'Worried, I'd say,' replied Thane, hanging up his coat and hat. 'He agrees that we've got to do something pretty drastic, and quickly, if this bird isn't going to disappear into thin air for all time.

'Incidentally, the Scientific Bureau have had no success

with those paint scrapings. They say they should be able to check the black upper coat if and when we find the bike, but that the red underneath was a cellulose composition used on several makes of machines about 1952.

'That brings me to our list of motorcycle owners. How's it getting on, Phil?'

Moss shook his head. 'They won't be finished work on it before tomorrow forenoon at the earliest, and there have been six men working round the clock on it for over thirty-six hours now. The big bother is that the Motor Taxation people don't file motorcycles separately. Their entire system is based on registration letters and numbers.

'There are something like a hundred thousand cars, lorries, buses and heaven knows what registered in Glasgow, and about seven thousand motorcycles are buried among the lot. Our men are having to dig out the bikes one at a time from the files, divide them into light and heavy machines, then finally make a list of the lightweight bike owners' addresses. The tax people are getting a bit peeved, too, for our lads can't avoid getting in their way.'

'It can't be helped,' insisted Thane. 'The Chief agreed with me that we'll need to start checking on every single bike in the city. I know, I know, it's a hell of a size of job. But it is the only way open to us. And remember, Phil, checking seven thousand bikes for scratches is nothing compared with some of the mass finger-printing searches that have been carried on in this country in recent years.

'The Chief is drafting extra help onto the job as soon as we can get started. Any bike with scratches which might have been caused in the hold-up or with new-looking paintwork recently applied is to be noted, the owner questioned. And it might not be such a big job, if we're lucky. I'm going to play a hunch that that bus ticket you found is a genuine lead. As soon as the list is near completion, we'll start on the Southwood area. It won't do any harm, as we have to start somewhere, and it may do an awful lot of good.

'Incidentally, I'm getting our photographers to run off about a hundred copies of the tyre tread we're looking for. It should be a help in trying to spot the bike we're after.'

'Bang goes my weekend off, though I must admit I thought it would be a miracle if I got away,' said Moss. 'While you were out I had the gentlemen of the press to deal with, by the way. Oh—and young David Renfield had a chat with me afterwards. He seems to be still a bit on edge after that blasting you gave him yesterday.'

'I should think so, too,' grinned Thane. 'Still, the youngster's all right. And he's a darned good reporter—when he isn't getting under my feet.'

The hard, slogging work of the murder hunt, dull and unglamorous, continued.

At almost the same moment as Thane, glancing up from his desk at the clock on the wall, decided it was time to have some sandwiches sent in for lunch, a scene which would have been of intense interest to him was taking place some sixty miles away.

The motorcycle which bore the vital scratches, clearly revealing a red coat of paint beneath black, had just been left under a hedge at the end of a bumpy hill path.

Its innocent, unsuspecting owner was beginning to heave, strain and sweat his way up a rain-lashed mountainside in his passion for open-air exercise.

CHAPTER TWENTY-THREE

BEFORE THE DAYS of the telephone, reporters had to make all their inquiries by personal visit, or, on occasion, written correspondence.

Their stories, if important enough, made their way back to the offices by telegraph, or even, on occasion, by carrier pigeon.

As far as the View office was concerned, however, the latter method went out of favour one Saturday afternoon when a pigeon, carrying the second-half report and final score of the main Scottish League football match of the day, being played at Hampden, only a few miles away, refused to land on the office dovecot.

Despite all coaxing, it fluttered and hopped from window ledge to window ledge, holding up the paper's production for nearly three-quarters of an hour before it decided that it would, after all, enter the pigeon loft.

But the telephone is now the all-important news-gathering instrument. Major happenings have been described by men who at the time were more than 300 miles away from the spot concerned, but who were prepared to sit with an opened telephone directory and pass call after call after call until they obtained the information they desired.

To gather the material for his proposed article on new precautions being taken by business firms, Renfield sat down at his desk with a cup of tea, a directory, and a packet of cigarettes. Then he began his phone bombardment.

Mr False Face, he discovered, had by stealing the Swivney payroll awakened several firms to the weaknesses of their own security measures in a way that succeeded where all the lectures read to the public over the years by successive Chief Constables had failed.

'We're changing things right away, old boy,' the manager of one large works assured him. 'You'll hardly believe it—and, of course. I'm sure you won't mention our name, bad publicity and all that—but we found that the payroll for this factory was actually collected from the bank each week by two of the typists, who walked there and back. Shocking! You'll appreciate I can't tell you what we are doing now—but we are taking no more chances like that!'

An insurance company had cause to be grateful for another reason. Business was booming for a combined policy in which they specialised, covering money, both on the move and kept overnight in offices, against the risk of theft.

The whole shaped nicely into a one-thousand-word article which he patiently shaped and polished most of that Saturday afternoon, ignoring the conditions around him as the Saturday night sports paper was produced in miraculous fashion from madhouse activity.

He finished his duty at five o'clock, ducked into a nearby restaurant for a meal, then, lacking a date with Jean, who was visiting a girlfriend, went along to the *Gaumont* and sat through a rip-roaring Technicolor Western.

After the usual catalogue of thrills, the cowboy drama

reached the evergreen climax. The chief goodie chased the chief baddie, the latter hiding behind a rock to shoot down the hero.

But, naturally, the gun was empty, and in the fist-fight which followed—goodies never shoot unarmed men—the baddie naturally fell over a cliff.

The wide-screen triumph of right over wrong pointed no particular moral to the reporter. Relaxed in the comfortable seat in the darkened cinema, he assessed his position.

Ignoring the ten-shilling notes, which he had to regard as so much wastepaper because of the possibility that they could be traced, he had £6,500 in worry-free cash. The police seemed to be floundering without the slightest idea where to turn.

'And Jean... I think she'll say yes,' he murmured. 'The way my luck's running she's almost bound to.'

Having seen the programme through, he decided on an early night, and drove home through the gaily lit, still busy streets.

Rain was starting to fall as he steered the Ford into its lock-up for the night. He hesitated inside the Nissen for a moment, then decided against digging the bag up from under the floor.

'The light, or the noise, might bring the local night-beat policeman snooping round,' he mused. 'There's no sense in taking the risk. I'll come along first thing in the morning and dig the stuff up. The ten-bob notes will have to be destroyed. The case will be more difficult, but I'll get rid of it as well.

'Lucky that that clown Dawkins will be shambling up and down his mountains until tomorrow evening. I'll be able to get the job done without any bother.'

Hearing his key in the front door lock, Mrs Senior, who had been considerably upset over his refusal to eat breakfast, fussed over him from the moment he entered her house. But she was quickly reassured by the way he tucked into supper.

'It was just a slight stomach upset I had,' he reassured her. 'I'm as fit as a horse again... and come to that, Mrs S., I could probably eat all the acceptable parts of one right now.'

He slept soundly.

Saturday night or not, there was no air of either relaxation or gaiety in the Motor Taxation offices in the centre of Glasgow. Behind drawn curtains, aided by the office staff, tired-eyed police continued drawing up their list of motorcycle owners.

At one desk sat a sergeant, who scrutinised each name and address as it was found, and placed any Southwood area registrations in a small but growing separate pile.

After an evening during which most of his time was taken up in sorting out the details of a stabbing case, the climax to a row at a more than somewhat drunken birthday party in a tenement only a stone's throw away from the police station, Thane finally had the last detail tied up and the knifeman in jail by about ten o'clock.

He took a trip along to the Taxation office to see how the work was progressing.

'With any luck and if we stay awake we'll be finished about breakfast tomorrow, sir,' reported the sergeant.

'Keep at it,' he ordered. 'The search is planned to start at 10 a.m. All squad car leave has been cancelled, and additional men are being drafted in. It's a slim chance that we'll find that bike. But at the moment it is our only hope.'

Shortly afterwards, being driven home in the C.I.D. duty car, Thane peered out through the rain-soaked windscreen while the twin wipers thrashed their monotonous song. All around him in the darkness lay row upon row of neat little houses.

Somewhere among them, totally unsuspected, perhaps, even by his own family, might be a man with a gun, a man who had killed once, and who might kill again.

He might be there... or he might not. He might be miles away, perhaps even out of the country altogether.

But, thought Thane, there was one very good reason for tomorrow's search, a reason which justified even the slenderest chance being taken. It lay in the red-brick city mortuary. Until Thursday afternoon it had been a cheery, resourceful young policeman named Macrae, whose ambition in life was to someday become a detective.

The bus ticket issued in Southwood might have been blown onto the waste ground where it had been found. It might, even if bought by the man they sought, have been taken out on a chance journey.

But the possibility was worth following up. And follow it up he would.

Mary had cocoa, biscuits, and his slippers ready by the fire for him when he arrived. They sat on opposite sides of the hearth, discussing the children's day, the weather... Anything except the murder hunt.

It was a rule they had established many years ago, one seldom broken, and one which Thane was often grateful for after a day spent battering his head against a particularly puzzling situation.

After a few minutes, however, he said, 'Mary, what's the food situation like for tomorrow? I think I may manage home for lunch, and I thought I'd bring Phil Moss back with me. We'll be working in this neighbourhood most of the day actually—there's a chance the bike used in the hold-up might have come from these parts.'

His wife smiled. 'If you don't bring Phil home tomorrow he's going to be very disappointed. He was on the phone about half an hour ago, just to ask how I was keeping, of course. Then he told me how much he admired my cooking, and did I know, by the way, that you'd both be over this way tomorrow! I couldn't do anything else but invite him. You know, I'm sure that landlady of his doesn't feed him well enough. She certainly doesn't seem to take any trouble to give him the things he needs with that bad stomach of his.'

'That means milk pudding again, I suppose,' groaned Thane in mock anger. 'Honestly, that fellow Moss can't be beaten for sheer brass neck...'

CHAPTER TWENTY-FOUR

IT WAS A DULL, grey morning, heavy clouds filling the sky, rain still falling steadily, when Renfield awoke.

Over breakfast he read the Sunday papers. The "Mr False Face" hunt was still page-one news, but comparatively little space was devoted to it, a sure sign of no important overnight development being known.

Going up to his room, he opened the suitcase, and once more took the automatic from beneath the bundle of clothes and put it in his pocket. On an impulse, he also extracted the spare magazines and shoved them into his hip pocket.

Then, pulling on his raincoat and jamming a soft hat on his head, he stepped out into the downpour, walking briskly along the road towards the lock-up.

There was no one in sight when he reached the vacant ground on which it and the huddle of other similar buildings stood.

Fumbling for a moment with the key, he unlocked the door and swung it open, dodging a small torrent of rainwater dislodged by the action. Carefully, he shut the door behind him again and locked it once more, deliberately leaving the key in the socket.

The shooting brake's handbrake was off. He went round to the front of the Ford and, both hands on the radiator, slowly pushed the vehicle backwards, one—two—three—four feet.

Then, nipping round to the driver's door, Renfield put on the handbrake and brought out the tyre lever from under the front seat. The portion of floor where the bag was buried now lay revealed. Swiftly the metal bar sank into the earth and ash, scraping away the top coating. Using his hands, the reporter scooped away the remainder.

Sitting back on his heels, he took off his hat and threw it carelessly onto the ground. There was the bag, black and now earth-stained, just as he had left it. With hands that trembled just a little, he opened the leather jaws and pushed one hand into the interior.

The physical satisfaction of feeling the hard, unyielding mass of banknotes within exhilarated him.

Renfield took the bag round to the car and, sitting in the rear seat, emptied the contents beside him and began sorting out the bundles, putting the ten-shilling notes into a small pile and the one-pound and other wads into a larger, constantly growing heap.

Then, above the patter of rain, magnified by the sound of its bouncing off the metal roof overhead, he heard another noise, a noise which sent his hand darting towards the automatic in his jacket pocket.

It was the pop-popping of a two-stroke motorcycle, a popping which rose in a sudden revving, then stopped altogether.

'My God!' he exclaimed aloud in his horror. 'It's Dawkins. What the hell's brought him back?'

A key grated into the lock, then stopped as it met his own key, which prevented the new arrival from operating the mechanism. There was a surprised moment's silence, then Dawkins' voice sang out, 'Hi, David, you in there? Let us in chum, the rain's lashing out here.'

His brain racing, Renfield began sweeping the bundles of notes onto the floor of the car. He shouted back, 'Hang on, John, I won't be a second. Just fixing something.' And as he did so, he threw the bag on top of the money and began feverishly stripping off his coat.

'Hey, come on, for Pete's sake,' came the voice again.

'All right, all right, I'm coming,' he replied, dumping his coat on the car floor and spreading it over the dynamite-like articles which lay beneath.

Renfield had stepped out of the car and was just about to go to the hut door when he remembered the hole in the garage floor. With a muttered curse and ignoring a thundering knocking and a shout from outside, he raced again to the driver's door, let off the handbrake, and, putting his shoulder to the windscreen pillar, heaved the car forward again until its nose was nearly touching the wall in front. The hole and the scattered earth were covered.

When, seconds later, he opened the door, a slightly irate John Dawkins was huddled against it, his one-piece weather suit black with rain.

'What the blazes were you up to, David? I might have drowned out there,' he complained as he wheeled his machine into the shelter.

'Sorry, but I was doing a repair job to the wiring. Remember that loose wire I mentioned yesterday, the one that kept me late for work? It gave a bit more trouble later on, shorting. I was busy taping it up and was halfway under the dashboard when you called,' lied Renfield with a fluency which surprised him. 'What brings you home, anyway? I thought you were staying up north until tonight?'

Dawkins, a look of disgust on his face, explained, unstrapping the bundle from the back of the *Dot*,

'It never stopped raining. I put up at the Youth Hostel overnight, but when I got up this morning and saw it still lashing down, well, this fellow decided he'd had enough. So here I am. Suppose I'd better away home now. I phoned Mum from the hostel to tell her there would be one more for lunch, so she'll be expecting me.

'Of course, if you need a hand with the car, I'll stay and help, you know.'

David Renfield hurriedly assured the eager young man that everything was now fine, and with a cheery wave, Dawkins plunged out into the rain again.

The man who had "just been mending a wire" leaned back against the car as soon as the motorcyclist disappeared. Heart thumping, legs trembling, he felt near to fainting.

Throughout the conversation he had kept his right hand in his jacket pocket, pressing against the automatic, ready to use it at an instant's notice.

Could he have mustered the resolve to use it? Strangely, he realised, he wouldn't have hesitated.

Was it because he had blood on his hands already? The vision of the dying policeman, the look on his face, the way he had slumped, rose before him. He gave a faint moan and buried his head in his hands.

Only after smoking a cigarette could he bring himself to move. The car had to be once more pushed back, the hole filled in. The money he packed back inside the bag, which he then hid at the rear of the Ford's spare wheel compartment.

On a sudden impulse he started the car, drove it out of the

garage, and headed south, out of town and into the country. Only on the moorland, with no one within miles, would he feel safe in checking his haul.

CHAPTER TWENTY-FIVE

AS THANE HAD PROMISED, the police search of the Southwood area began just after 10 a.m.

Eight Jaguar cars, withdrawn from normal patrol duty for the purpose, crawled from house to house through the driving rain in their systematic hunt.

Each crew had drawn a list of names and addresses as they set off. They charted their progress through the main police radio station at Cathkin Braes to a temporary headquarters set up in a radio-equipped Black Maria patrol van parked in a street in the centre of the area.

Several of the motorcyclists on their lists were not at home, either at church or out for the day. Their names were ticked for a later call. But others were found in their houses, many enjoying a Sunday morning long lie in bed.

They were politely requested to show licences and insurance certificates, and then asked to allow their motorcycles to be inspected.

There was consternation in one household, where the owner of one little machine, pop-popping up to his door with the Sunday papers almost at the same time as the police drew up, was found to be neither insured nor in possession of a Road Fund licence.

Another rider, in a newer part of the suburb, didn't wait for the police to speak, but admitted right away that he had "fiddled" a quantity of bricks from a nearby builder's lot... and please, would it be all right if he just carted them back again?

But, although machines were found with crumpled mudguards, and scraped paintwork, no bike answering the "black with red showing through" description could be found in the first two hours.

'Car Three calling Control. We have located possible machine. Will you please inform headquarters to proceed to No. 28 Garette Street, repeat No. 28 Garette Street, where we are holding the owner for interview?'

Moss, who had been waiting with Thane at the Black Maria, was on his way aboard the duty C.I.D. car within seconds of the message being relayed.

No. 28 Garette Street was a tidy little mid-terrace house of red sandstone. Two police cars were already drawn up outside it, and as Moss left the Sunbeam and went towards the house door it opened, and a uniform sergeant came to meet him.

'We've got him in the lounge, Inspector,' he reported. 'His name is John Dawkins, and he took us round to see the bike himself. He admits the scratches, but says they were caused by some accident in the lock-up where he keeps it.'

'Red paint under the black?' queried Moss.

'Yes,' nodded the sergeant. 'And I had a look at the tyres as well. I'm not an expert, of course, sir, but the rear wheel tread looks awfully like the sample in the photograph we were issued with.'

He showed Moss into the lounge, where a red-faced flustered Dawkins sat on a couch beside a middle-aged woman.

'Look, mister,' he exclaimed. 'This whole business is crazy. I can explain...'

Moss stopped him in mid-sentence.

'We are only making certain inquiries, Mr Dawkins. There is no need to become upset—at this stage.'

The woman spoke. 'My son hasn't done anything wrong. The police won't even tell us what it is all about. What is going on? His father's out at church just now and won't be back for about another hour.'

'My name is Moss. I'm an inspector in the Criminal Investigation Department of Millside Police. A policeman was shot, and a cashier robbed of a large sum of money on Thursday afternoon. The man responsible escaped on a motorcycle,' replied the policeman.

'We are checking on all motorcycles in this area, Mrs Dawkins, and it happens that the machine belonging to your son has certain peculiarities about it which we would like to have explained.'

The woman sat silent, white-faced. Her son's eyes had widened in horror.

'Now then, Mr Dawkins, perhaps you can tell us how these scratches came to be on the machine... but first,' nodding towards the police sergeant, who stood, notebook ready, 'I must warn you that anything you say will be taken down in writing and may be used in evidence.'

The youngster waved aside the formal words of caution.

'Of course I can tell you about them. But look, this hold-up was on Thursday afternoon, wasn't it? Well, I was with my boss and half a dozen other people all afternoon. I couldn't have had anything to do with the robbery.

'As for the scratches, they're easily explained. The chap whose lock-up I share—we've only got a tiny toolshed in the back garden here—dropped the bike when he was moving it yesterday morning to get his car out. He'll tell you all about it. In fact, we joked at the time about the police stopping me... though I never dreamed that it would actually happen.'

Moss tapped his foot. 'This man who dropped the machine. What's his name and address?'

'David Renfield. He's a reporter who stays quite near here,' replied Dawkins.

Moss relaxed a little, his voice became more friendly. 'We'll make immediate inquiries into this,' he told the young motorcyclist. 'Meantime, give me the name of your employer, will you, and his home address if you know it.'

Dawkins eagerly provided the details.

Moss turned towards his mother. 'I'm sorry, Mrs Dawkins, I'm afraid I'll have to ask your son to remain here for the present. And a police escort will have to stay in the house. However, if what your son says is true—and it looks as though we should be able to confirm what he says pretty quickly—he has absolutely nothing to worry about.'

Leaving the mother and son still seated, gazing dumbly at one another, he went out into the hallway. There, turning to the sergeant who had followed him from the room, he instructed, 'Keep a close eye on him. I'll send a couple of extra men along. You haven't moved the motorcycle yet, have you?'

The sergeant shook his head.

'Then I'll get the patrol van to pick it up and take it for examination,' continued Moss. 'The men can also run the rule over the lock-up, and we'll leave a man on duty there for the time being.'

'What do you think of his story, sir?'

'Difficult to say. He seems to be speaking the truth, though the similarity of the bike will take a bit of explaining. I know this reporter Renfield he mentioned. He's working on the case for his paper. We'll see him, and, of course, get in touch with

Dawkins' boss right away. Well, I'd better go along to the boss and see what he says about it all.'

The inspector's car took only a few minutes to return to where the patrol van waited. Thane listened intently to Moss's report.

'We'll go round right now and take a look at this motorbike and the lock-up,' he commented. 'I'll get Sergeant MacLean to locate Dawkins' boss and have a word with him. And it might be as well for him to go round and get hold of young Renfield and see what he has to say about all this. It would serve Renfield right if we really put the wind up him and asked just where he was on Thursday.'

Followed by the patrol van, they drove round to the Nissen hut lock-up, and Moss, who had collected the door key from the sergeant before he left the Dawkins' home, opened up the makeshift garage. The *Dot* stood alone in one corner, only in the marks of car wheel-tracks in the ash floor testifying to another vehicle using the hut.

Thane peered at the machine's paintwork, scratched and chipped. His face was grim. Then, taking the photographic copy of the missing bike's tyre tread from his pocket, he examined the *Dot's* wheels.

At last he stood up. 'It's up to the Scientific Branch,' he declared. 'But if this isn't the one, it's damn like it.'

Moss had been prowling around the garage, scuffing his feet on the ashes. Suddenly he stopped, looking at the peculiar streaks of brown earth which had suddenly appeared on his shoes. He bent down.

'Colin! Take a look at this,' he exclaimed. 'The earth here... it's loose, almost as if somebody's been digging.'

Thane joined him, and taking a pencil from his waistcoat pocket, prodded the small area indicated.

'You're right. And do you notice anything about the size? Just big enough to take, say, a bag.'

He turned towards the door. 'Constable!' The uniformed man who had been waiting by the entrance came forward.

'Get a message through to the Scientific Branch for me, will you? Tell them I want them to come out here, examine the shed and this ash floor, particularly at this spot, and to take the bike to Headquarters for a full examination. I don't like the look of this. Phil, leave MacLean to locate Dawkins' boss. But go round yourself and see if you can find young Renfield. It's time we had a word with him.'

Left alone in the shed, Thane stared moodily at the motorcycle, mentally doodling as he sought to avoid the sudden conclusions which were dancing through his mind.

Young Renfield had a Ford shooting brake. He stayed in Southwood. Motorcycles... The policeman suddenly remembered a snatch of conversation he had exchanged with the reporter one morning when he was being given a lift into town.

A motorcyclist had cut sharply in front of them, and Renfield had had to brake savagely to avoid collision.

"When I was a despatch rider, the instructor would have thrown a fit if I'd tried a stunt like that," Renfield had said.

As soon as the laboratory crew had arrived and he had described to them what he wanted done, Thane hurried to the nearest telephone box and called the Evening View office.

It being a Sunday, none of the View staff were on duty, but a reporter on the View's morning companion, the Bugle, gave him the View news editor's home phone number.

A child's voice answered when he rang the Bearsden number he had been given. He heard a piping shout of 'Daddy' and then McRowder, the news editor, spoke.

'Sorry for the delay; I was up in the loft tidying up some

stuff. Who is this speaking? Hello, Mr Thane. What can I do for you?'

The detective asked, 'I can't explain what this is all about, and it isn't for publication. But can you tell me if your reporter Renfield was at work on Thursday?'

McRowder chuckled. 'No, it was his day off. I was cursing at the time, you know, over that payroll job. Right up his street, professionally speaking. Here, what's he been up to anyway?'

'Nothing, I hope,' replied Thane. 'We're just making some inquiries and someone's mentioned his name. Nothing to worry about.'

He hung up, eyes bleak, and, moving quickly, returned to the Nissen hut.

Mr David Renfield was going to have a few very awkward questions to answer in the immediate future.

CHAPTER TWENTY-SIX

DULL GREY RAIN clouds were once more rolling threateningly across the sky when, far out on a narrow, windswept moorland road, more than twenty miles from Glasgow, the Ford brake finally slowed and halted; nearside wheels high on the grass verge so that if another vehicle should come along it could pass without fuss or trouble.

Except for a few crows, their black wings flapping lazily through the air, and a solitary seagull, startlingly white, there was no sign of life in all the bleak, rolling miles of waterlogged heath and bracken which lay all around.

Killing the engine, Renfield permitted himself a few moments' relaxation before, sliding from behind the driving wheel, he got down to the business which had brought him to this desolate spot. Bringing out the money-crammed bag, he emptied its contents and swiftly, as if dealing with so many packs of playing cards, separated the bundles of ten-shilling notes from the other, completely safe banknotes.

Putting the useless, dangerous paper back into the leather bag, he took another glance around the bleak, still empty moorland, then, satisfied by his scrutiny, stepped from the car. Searching in the wet grassland, Renfield selected several large stones, which he packed into the bag until it was brimful. Then he walked across the squelching ground, away from the road. After a few hundred yards he found what he wanted, a patch of deep, watery bog-land, marked by its tufts of dark green vegetation.

Taking the topmost stone from the bag, he threw it into the centre of the patch, and watched it immediately disappear beneath the surface. Then, with a quick, strong heave, Renfield sent the bag after it. The weighted leather landed with a "plop" on the surface, and for a moment appeared as if it would remain there. But slowly at first, then more quickly, it too slid under, a sudden gout of bubbles being the last indication of its presence before the mud once more smoothed into shape.

Hastening back over the moorland to the Ford, the reporter carefully packed the remaining bundles of money into an old Army respirator haversack, a khaki reminder of his National Service days.

Banknotes are surprisingly bulky. Despite his putting another thick wad of one-pound notes into his pocket, the loaded haversack, containing in the region of £6,500, was well filled and had become quite heavy.

Humming a little tune to himself, he stowed the haversack away in the hiding place at the back of the spare wheel compartment, then, content, took out a cigarette and flicked his lighter.

There were sparks, but no flame. It needed petrol. Stuffing the cigarette into his jacket handkerchief pocket, he shrugged his shoulders, moved into the driving seat, switched on the ignition, and a few minutes later was driving off along the road.

A mile or so on he passed a farm lorry, pounding on its way

with a full load amid a cloud of stinking diesel smoke. The two drivers exchanged cheery waves.

A hotel situated at the corner where the moorland road joined a broad trunk artery was Renfield's goal. It was nearly two o'clock, but the proprietor, delighted to see any custom at this quiet time of the year, promised to "see what he could find" for lunch.

He "found" a meal which left Renfield satisfied but sleepy, and after a quiet drink in the lounge bar, it was almost a struggle to leave the warmth of the hotel and walk to the car park, where the Ford lay in solitary splendour.

Lighting a cigarette—he had coaxed a refill for his lighter from the barmaid—he headed back towards Glasgow, the damp afternoon air seeming to make the Ford's engine run with a new smooth purring power.

'The next car I buy is going to have a radio fitted,' he mused. 'Could do with a nice spot of music right now. Wonder how many radios I could buy with the little lot I've got stored in the boot? Well over three hundred, I suppose.

'Sorry, Mr Thane, but this looks like one little job that will have to go down as "unsolved" in the next police annual report.'

He drew up at an A.A. box on the fringe of the city, and telephoned Jean's home.

'Well, hello stranger,' mocked her voice when she answered. 'Do you realise I haven't seen you in nearly forty-eight hours?'

'I'll mend that quickly enough,' he promised her. 'Could I pick you up in the car and we'll go out for tea somewhere? Say five o'clock? And afterwards we could go for a run along a nice dark road I know!'

'How dark?' she asked, then agreed, 'All right, but I'll need to be back fairly early. I've a heavy day ahead of me tomorrow.

It may be winter, but this is the time of year when the buyers start looking for swimsuits for next season, and Mr Rabinski has asked me to help a friend of his by modelling a collection of them.'

Renfield gave a low wolf-whistle, then chuckled as the receiver at the other end banged down. He glanced at his watch. It was just leaving half past three.

Down the road a little he pulled in at a garage, had the tank refilled with petrol, the tyres and oil checked, and chatted with the mechanic for a while.

Still killing time, he stopped at a little roadside cafe and, over coffee and another cigarette, read a couple of Sunday papers left lying by a previous patron.

It was nearly four-thirty when he drove into Southwood, heading for his lodgings and a quick wash and brush up before he collected Jean at her home.

Then, in the gathering dusk, just beginning to be lit by the clear, orange glare of the streetlights, he saw the two Black cars —police cars—drawn up outside the row of terrace buses he was passing... the row in which John Dawkins stayed.

Renfield struggled against the lightning impulse to ram his foot hard down on the accelerator. Instead, he kept his steady, 30-mile-an-hour course, and the policeman sitting in the smaller car—one of the new *Sunbeams* recently acquired by the Glasgow Force, a corner of his mind registered—didn't even bother to look up.

He drove on, no longer towards his home, but on a vague, slow, aimless course.

"What on earth were they doing there?" he asked himself. "Could they have...? Surely they couldn't possibly have traced the motorcycle.

"Maybe Dawkins has been in an accident. Or something could have happened at the house."

But he knew the coincidence was too great to be probable. Yet surely Thane couldn't be looking for him, or the policeman in the car wouldn't have let him pass so easily?

Like many a man before him, he cursed himself for underrating Thane. There was only one way to make sure, and that was to go on to the lock-up.

He drew the Ford into the roadside a little way away from the avenue in which the Nissen was situated, nervously plucked at his pocket for the gun which nestled there, then, feeling its reassuring bulk, got out and walked to the corner.

In the grey dusk the avenue appeared empty. Glimpses of light from behind drawn curtains showed that most of the householders were settling down indoors. Somewhere a radio was blaring.

But he couldn't see the garage. It was set a little back from the road, and a high privet hedge in the garden next to it blocked his view.

Renfield walked down the pavement, still dark and wet from a recent rain shower, his every step seeming to echo and re-echo in the silence.

Nearly opposite the garage... nearly... Now! He took a quick glance. A policeman was standing patiently beside the closed door of the Nissen, a just discernible figure in the gloom.

"Keep walking... slowly... don't panic," he told himself. His steps remained steady. There was no shout, no shrill whistle.

It took probably five seconds to cross the entry and be lost to the view of the man in the dark blue uniform coat. It seemed like five years in terms of suspense.

Turning left at the next corner, then left again, he returned to the Ford. Less than five minutes had elapsed. Automatically, Renfield started the engine, let in the clutch, jerked away from the kerb and drove down the road.

How much did Thane know? How had they traced the bike... for that could be the only explanation of the cars outside its owner's home, the guard at the garage. What, above all, should he do? Should he stay and bluff, or run?

"Perhaps it's just a formal check," he pondered. "But would they leave a guard on the lock-up on a mere routine search?"

Once more, but in a totally different state of mind, he stopped the car to make a telephone call. Slipping into the call-box, he quickly dialled his landlady's number. The ringing tone had hardly started when the telephone at the other end was answered by Mrs Senior.

'Hello, Mrs S.,' he said, trying to keep his voice level and untroubled. 'Just wondering if there had been any messages?'

'Oh, David, I'm so glad you called,' she replied, voice nervous and obviously agitated. 'A policeman has been round twice looking for you. He said he'd come back later. And Mr McRowder, your news editor, was on the telephone. He was wondering where you were, and he seemed awfully anxious to trace you.

'You haven't been in an accident with the car, or got yourself into some kind of trouble, have you?'

'Everything's all right, Mrs Senior,' he reassured her. 'I'll take care of the messages. Tell me, did the policeman give his name?'

'Yes, he was an inspector, he said, a Mr Moss. He wouldn't say what it was about at all, just that he wanted to see you.'

Renfield hung up, a fresh wave of apprehension sweeping over him. The decision had been taken. Run.

Get back into the car and drive away.

No, that was useless. Probably the police radio was even then beginning to pump out details of his car to the forces of every county in Scotland and the North of England.

The car was as useful as a six-foot-high neon sign.

Quickly he got inside it, started the engine, and drove into the nearest side street. Renfield parked the vehicle beside two other cars, drawn up without lights outside the row of bungalows.

Stopping only to put out his own lights and take the haversack of money from the hiding-place, he walked rapidly away.

Shivering in the damp night air, he waited at a nearby stop until a bus came along, boarded it, and sat downstairs, mind racing over a dozen possible escape plans and rejecting each just as quickly as possible.

There was Ireland. But the boats would be watched.

London? He remembered the long, long procession of men he had seen marching through the courts on their way to long terms in prison after being picked up in the capital.

The Continent? How could he get there?

The Highlands, wild and lonely? Up there at this time of the year a stranger stood out like a sore thumb.

A twinge shot through him as, glancing at the khaki haversack under his arm, he recalled how it was to have smoothed his path with Jean.

Jean... he had to see her before he went away. She might come with him. She might.

Renfield left the bus at the next stop, walked across the road, and boarded a bus that would take him towards Pollokshields.

CHAPTER TWENTY-SEVEN

RENFIELD HAD BEEN RIGHT on one count, wrong on another, when, on seeing the cars outside Dawkins' home, he had decided the police were now after him. Thane was looking for him. But at that stage, he had not yet sufficient proof to make his search one for an escaping murderer, though that came swiftly afterwards.

The Chief Inspector arrived back at the Nissen lock-up after his telephone conversation with McRowder, the View news editor, at almost the same time as Moss returned in the squad car.

The inspector emerged from the car shaking his head. 'No luck, I'm afraid. I saw the landlady, but she says she hasn't the slightest idea where he is. She thinks Renfield's gone off somewhere in his car but doesn't know when he will be back or where he's likely to have gone to.'

'Let's get round to Dawkins' home then,' suggested Thane. 'I want to hear that lad's story. Then I want to try and get this thing straight in my head. A lot of things have happened that I'm not at all happy about.'

At the little terrace house, they found the motorcyclist still sitting in the lounge, now joined by his father, who, just returned from church, came towards them, an angry look on his face.

'Well,' he demanded. 'Have you found out now what a big mistake you're making about my lad? There will be trouble over this, I warn you.'

'Trouble over what, Mr Dawkins?' asked Thane wearily. 'Your son is in an awkward position, and carrying on like that won't help things. Understand this, Mr Dawkins. We are trying to check on your son's story of his movements on Thursday afternoon. But his motorcycle bears certain marks, and the tyre tread is also almost identical with one we found after the Swivney robbery.'

'But, damn it, my son wouldn't do that kind of thing. He isn't a killer.'

'No father ever thinks his son is, Mr Dawkins,' said Thane. 'I hope your son isn't. But we have to make our inquiries. Right now, I want to ask him a few more questions.'

He introduced himself to the young rider, who almost whispered his acknowledgement.

'Look, son, I need some information from you. Help me, and you're helping yourself. Where was your bike on Thursday afternoon?'

'In the lock-up. It's always there through the week,' said Dawkins.

'Could anybody else get at it then? Anyone at all? Even your father or mother?'

The crop of red hair shook in a negative. 'I've got the only key. The only other person that could get in would be the fellow I share the garage with, David Renfield. And he wouldn't need the bike. He's got his car.'

'But he could get at it?' persisted Thane. 'Do you know whether he can ride motorcycles?'

'Oh, he can ride them, that's true,' agreed Dawkins. 'He was a despatch rider or something in the Army. David's had a couple of spins on the bike, just to keep his hand in. But I told the inspector already, it couldn't have been my *Dot*. The scratches on it happened when David dropped it yesterday morning.'

'All of them?' asked Thane. 'Did you see the bike before it was dropped?'

'No...' Dawkins began, when a constable slipped into the room and whispered to Thane.

The Chief Inspector excused himself, and went out into the hallway, where Detective Sergeant MacLean was waiting.

'Hello, sir. I got round to Dawkins' employer. He confirmed every word about that lunch party on the Thursday, and says Dawkins was kept busy till after four o'clock.'

Thane re-entered the lounge, strode over to the couch, and looked down at Dawkins.

'You can relax, son. Your boss confirms your story.'

Dawkins jumped to his feet, eyes blinking back sudden tears of relief, while his father came round beside him.

Thane went on, 'There is still the mystery of your bike to clear up, however. Maybe Mr Renfield can throw some light on that.'

'Why don't you find him then?' snapped the elder Dawkins.

'We're trying to do that right now,' Thane assured him. 'Just for now, however, he can't be found. And Mr Dawkins, you'll appreciate that your son's bike has been taken to Police Headquarters for examination and may have to remain there a little while.'

He retired from the room as Mr Dawkins prepared a fresh

assault. Moss was waiting in the hallway and fell into step as he walked towards the door.

Thane snapped his fingers. 'Mary—I've just remembered. She'll still be waiting on us coming home for that meal. Look, Phil, I tell you what to do. Take another scout up to Renfield's lodgings. See if you can snatch a picture of him from anywhere.'

'Then we'll meet at your place...' suggested Moss.

'No time,' disagreed his chief. 'I'll look in and apologise to Mary. Anyway, as I was saying, you go to his lodgings. If he isn't there, leave a couple of men on watch. Tell them to go somewhere where they can't be seen, but from which they can keep the house under observation. If Renfield returns, they've to contact us immediately, then ask him to come along for questioning.

'You join me back at Millside as soon as you can. We've got work to do—and I've a few surprising things to tell you.'

There was still no word from the reporter when Moss once more called on an increasingly worried Mrs Senior. She became even more worried when the inspector asked if she had a photograph of her lodger, but finally produced a quite reasonable snapshot, taken in the back garden of her home that summer.

Leaving the two plain-clothes men posted inconspicuously some little distance away, Moss returned to Millside.

'I'd give a lot to know where he is right now,' growled Thane. 'I've just been on to the Scientific Bureau, but their report on the motorcycle isn't complete yet. Let's see the picture, Phil.'

He placed the snapshot on his desk and stared at it for a

moment. Then, with a sudden exclamation, he pulled open the top drawer of his desk, rifled through the papers within, and pulled out a second picture.

Laying the two side by side, he gave a long, low whistle.

'Take a look,' he invited. 'Then give me a damn good kick. On your right, Danny O'Farrell, on your left, David Renfield.'

The two pictures held Moss's eyes for a long minute. Then he looked up. 'They could pass in a crowd for one another,' he agreed. 'Why didn't we see it before?'

'Because although we've seen them both, we know them too well to even think of them looking alike until we see it in picture form,' exclaimed Thane. He stood up. 'Come on, Phil. No time to eat yet. We're going off to see young Wheeler and show him these two pictures.'

The mechanic was out when they called at his home in Springburn. But his mother directed the two detectives to a local cafe, where they found him deeply engrossed in the attractions of a pretty little brunette.

'Mind if we join you?' asked Thane and, taking the surprised look as agreement, pulled in a chair to the little table. 'Hello, Miss, won't keep the lad more than a couple of minutes.'

At the cafe counter, Moss was hurriedly organising two cups of coffee and a plate of biscuits. As he came over with them, the Chief Inspector had just laid the two pictures down on the tabletop.

'Take a close look at them,' he invited. 'Tell me if you recognise anybody.'

'I made a big enough fool of myself the last time,' grumbled Wheeler. But he bent over the photographs, while the two policemen sipped their coffee and munched a biscuit.

'This one'—pointing to the picture of O'Farrell—'this is the bloke I picked out before.' He stared at the second photograph, then suddenly snorted.

'This is him. Really, no kidding. The other fellow looked like the bloke I saw. But this is the real one.' He stopped, suddenly puzzled. 'I've seen him somewhere else, though.'

Thane and Moss sat still, not uttering a word or changing their disinterested expressions.

When Wheeler looked up again his face was pink, he said a word which brought a startled protest from his girlfriend. 'What a ruddy mug I've been,' he spluttered. 'It's that reporter, isn't it?'

Thane scooped up the photographs. 'That's all for just now,' he said. 'But we'll be back.'

With a protesting, biscuit-chewing Moss trailing in his wake, he left the little cafe and got back into the police car waiting outside.

'Renfield's lodgings in Southwood,' he instructed the driver. 'Now listen to this, Phil.'

He began to sketch his discoveries, beginning with his talk with the reporter's news editor.

Moss sat spellbound, then, as he finished, exclaimed, 'So now we pick him up!'

'When we find him,' corrected Thane. 'And even then, we'll have to fill in a few more blank spaces before we can be completely sure.'

Their car drew up outside Mrs Senior's home, and the two men went up to the door. The landlady opened it to their knock.

'Any word yet, Mrs Senior?' asked Moss.

'He's telephoned me,' admitted the landlady. 'He said he'd get in touch with you. Haven't you heard from him yet?'

Moss slowly shook his head. 'I'm afraid Mr Renfield is in a

rather serious spot of trouble, Mrs Senior,' he said. 'Have there been any other telephone calls?'

'His young lady was on the telephone, too, sir,' stammered Mrs Senior. 'She was properly annoyed. She said David—Mr Renfield, that is—was to have visited her half an hour ago.'

Mrs Senior didn't know Jean's address. A glance at a telephone directory, however, revealed that.

Ordering the two watchers to come from their posts into the house and instructing them to detain Renfield if he appeared, Thane swept round by car to the Catta home.

Miss Catta herself, light of battle in her eyes, answered the door.

'Well, about time—Oh, I'm sorry. I thought it was someone else,' she apologised.

'Mr Renfield?' suggested Thane. 'I'd like to talk to you about him if I may. You're Jean, aren't you?'

Frowning, the girl nodded, then asked angrily, 'How does it concern you?'

He quietly showed his warrant card. It had, for once, little effect.

'If David Renfield's got himself into trouble, it's no concern of mine,' she declared. 'I know nothing that can possibly be of interest to you.'

Her father's voice interrupted, 'What's no concern, lass? Who is this gentleman?'

Thane once more introduced himself. Dr Catta, in off-duty dress of flannels and pullover, waved him into the house, and Jean flounced in their wake into the front room.

'Sit down, sit down, Chief Inspector,' invited Dr Catta. 'What can we do for you, eh?'

'It's really your daughter who may be able to help,' he replied. 'Miss Catta, I believe you were to have been picked up by David Renfield this evening?'

Her father chuckled. 'Sorry, Inspector, but she's been raging about for nearly an hour, wondering where he's got to. That lad's got a warm reception awaiting him. But what's it got to do with the police? Has he been hurt or something?' His voice became more serious in tone.

'As far as I know, Doctor, there's nothing wrong with his health,' replied Thane. 'I'd like to ask your daughter, though, if she has seen him at all in the last few days. We're just making certain inquiries into one or two things.'

Jean stared sulkily for a moment, then admitted, 'I saw him on Thursday night, and then on Friday night. That isn't a crime, is it?'

Thane kept his patience with an effort.

'No, it isn't a crime, miss. But obstructing the police can be. Now, I want you to tell me if you've noticed anything unusual about him of late. Has he been spending his money rather freely, for instance?'

Jean raised her eyebrows. 'Just what are you getting at?'

'Answer the inspector, Jean, and none of your damn nonsense,' snapped her father. 'I don't understand this, but obviously something's wrong, and it is our duty to help.'

The girl's shoulders fell. 'Well, he sometimes is generous,' she admitted. 'But then, he's a gentleman'—she glared—'and doesn't make a song about it.'

'I'll say he spends money,' Doctor Catta supplemented. 'David's bought her several expensive presents which must have set him back a few pounds. And as recently as Friday night they had a gay time in Edinburgh. Jean said he had a wad of money. When I was his age, I'm damned if I could afford that sort of thing. I'd say he was a bit of a fool with his money.

'Here, was it his?'

'I'm sorry,' said Thane. 'I can't say anything more just now. I may be up to see you again. And I'd appreciate it, Doctor, if you'd telephone the police if young Renfield tries to get in touch with your daughter again.'

He left the house. Back in the car, he radioed a request for a couple of men to be sent to watch the Catta flat from cover. With the acknowledgement of the message came a request for him to go to the Scientific Bureau at Police Headquarters.

It took the car twenty minutes to cover the distance. At the laboratory, where white-coated workers were busy on half a dozen tasks, the motorcycle, much of it dusted in fingerprint powder, stood in one corner.

Superintendent Nichols, a gleam of triumph in his eye, met Thane as he entered the room.

'We've got something here all right, Colin,' he declared. 'This motorcycle is definitely the one we want. The tyres have unmistakably the same characteristics as the marks left in the lane. Paint samples from it match up exactly, both in colour and chemical content, with the scrapings from the roadway. It's as near definite as dammit.'

Thane, eyes grim, thanked the Superintendent and went over to the little room where the Chief Detective Superintendent, head of all Glasgow's C.I.D., was still on duty.

When he emerged ten minutes later, he headed straight for the operations centre.

'I want a general call out, both radio and teleprinter, for a silver-grey Ford shooting brake, the driver a reporter called David Renfield,' he told the officer in charge. 'The car is to be stopped, the occupant detained. Warn our men to be careful. Renfield is probably armed, and is wanted on suspicion of being involved in the Swivney payroll shooting.'

He gave details of the car and a brief description of Renfield. Then, leaving the snapshot photograph with the operations man, and promising to send in a larger one as quickly as possible, he went back out to his waiting car and instructed the driver to return to Renfield's lodgings, where Moss would be waiting for him.

On the way they passed Thane's bungalow. The children's bedrooms were already in darkness, but a faint light glowed from the sitting-room window.

"Mary's watching TV," he thought ruefully. "What was it she said was on? A good murder mystery play."

He would have given quite a lot to have been comfortably settled at the fireside with her. Instead, he was just setting the machinery in motion for the pursuit of a killer, who, just at that moment, might have been anywhere in Scotland.

Thane thought once more of the young policeman's grief-stricken mother. He murmured softly, 'We'll get him for you. And if he's the one, he'll suffer.'

CHAPTER TWENTY-EIGHT

DAVID RENFIELD CAUGHT a bus which took him to within a few hundred yards of Atlight Road, then, after a few minutes' indecision, telephoned the Catta home from a call-box. He was in luck. Jean herself answered the telephone.

'Jean,' he said hoarsely, 'I must see you. I'm in a jam. I want to explain what's happening.'

'Don't bother,' came her voice, cold and distant. 'A policeman has just been round looking for you. We're supposed to let him know if you try to get in touch with us. What on earth is going on? What did you do, and how did you drag my name into it?'

'I—I can't explain it on the phone, Jean. Look, will you come and meet me? I can straighten all this out. You were the reason for what I did. I'm not very far from your house now. I don't want to come over, as it's probably being watched. But will you try to come to see me?' he pleaded.

Her voice almost a hiss of anger, Jean Catta snapped, 'No. The detective said you'd stolen money. You'll go to jail, and if you think I'm having anything to do with a jailbird, you're mistaken. Yet you had the absolute effrontery to ask me to marry you. You—you damned brute. I won't come to see you. I won't lift a finger to help you. And if you dare to telephone this house again, I'll tell Mr Thane immediately.'

She hung up. Anger boiled up in a blind rage inside Renfield as he slowly replaced his receiver.

The rotten little bitch. The cheap little, dirty little...

She didn't matter a damn anymore. She was unimportant. But he still had the money. He could buy a dozen like her with it. Only one thing counted now, getting clear. He had to get right out of the country. And the quickest way to do that was by air.

As the red mist of anger cleared in his mind, a plan began to form. First, he had to steal a car. Then he had to get to Prestwick, Scotland's international airport.

There are many ways to break into even the most carefully locked car with the minimum of fuss. The older the car, the easier the method.

A window can be broken. A door handle can be forced by a hard blow. Some windows will slide open against their mechanism at the downward pressure of a gloved palm.

Many cars even have the number of their opening key stamped on the outside of a door handle, a key which can be bought for a few pence anywhere, without questions being asked.

Scores of other cars have been stolen by simply opening unlocked boots, climbing inside, pushing the back seat squab forward, and gaining access to the controls.

The fugitive chose the simplest way of all. First, however, he decided to get clear of the Atlight Road area. He hopped on a bus going into town, and stayed on it until it had crossed the city and was once more beginning to head out towards the suburbs which lay beyond.

On foot once more, he walked along several streets, selecting his target with care. Finally, he decided on a small pre-war Hillman Minx, one of a row of locked vehicles parked in a lane flanking a church in which a service appeared to be in progress. Only one dim streetlamp cast a glow over the area.

Taking out his penknife, Renfield deliberately broke the smaller blade off short, and used the remaining stub as a screw-driver to loosen the two screws on the plate holding the driver's handle in position. It took only half a minute to draw out the screws, then, as he shook the door handle, the lock swung back and the door opened.

He climbed inside, feeling blindly with his fingertips for the ignition switch. As he found it, he used the penknife again. This time its other blade, gently inserted, operated the worn ignition lock.

The starter motor seemed to wheeze with a noise like a steam-roller. But the engine fired, and he quickly but quietly drove away.

"North," he told himself. "That's the way to go. North first, then dump this car where it can be easily found, get another and swing south again, back towards Prestwick. That'll draw them off the track."

He drove carefully, eyes constantly watching for police, and as soon as possible turned off the main highway on the start of a maze of side roads which would take him slowly, but surely, northwards; a route which would take double the time of the direct road, but which would be ten times safer from police patrols.

After just over half an hour's driving he was lost. But, shining the flame of his cigarette lighter round the interior of the Hillman—the roof light was out of action—he found a folded map stuffed into one of the door pockets, painfully traced his route, and once more set off. Another hour passed before he reached his goal, the small town of Larbert.

"I'll ditch this rattletrap here," he told himself.

Renfield parked the Hillman, sidelights blazing, in the main street only a short distance away from the town's railway station.

As he got out of the car and moved along the pavement a laughing group of teenagers walked past, sparing not a glance in his direction.

He set off down the road. A policeman stood at the corner, checking the door of a tobacconist's shop, shut for the night.

'Cold night,' greeted Renfield, walking past. 'Aye,' agreed the man. 'And there's rain on the way, sir.'

On down the road he went, slowing as he saw a car park set to one side off the road, a mere patch of waste ground but packed with vehicles.

Their owners were probably in one or other of the local hotels, enjoying a quiet Sunday drink. He glanced at his watch. Nine o'clock. With luck, it would be another half hour and more before the cry of 'Time, gentlemen,' chased the motorists back out to their cars.

'Half an hour,' he muttered. 'That's long enough to get clear. Now, unless there's an attendant...'

His hand went into his pocket, fingers curling round the automatic and dragging it almost clear of the cloth. He stepped off the pavement and into the car park.

Ears strained to catch the slightest sound of anyone coming towards the car park, he moved swiftly down the rows of parked vehicles. There was no attendant to be seen.

This time he selected a speedy little T.R.2—just what Jean had wanted, he thought bitterly. It was standing in the middle of the second row, and this time he didn't have to try the penknife trick.

Like most sports cars, the T.R.2 had no thief-proof lock on its doors, and the side screen unbuttoned in a flash. And, again like most sports cars, it had no ignition lock, merely an on-off switch.

Muting the powerful engine as best he could, Renfield drove out of the park. Exhaust quietly burbling, the two-seater purred along the road, heading north once more.

But as soon as the town was passed he changed direction, turning up a minor road on the start of a huge semi-circular sweep which would take him southeast, then-southwest, and finally towards Prestwick Airport.

The Triumph had plenty of petrol. It had power to spare.

A confident, sneering grin began to return to the fugitive's face.

A trampled litter of cigarette stubs on the brown rubber floor covering marked the passage of time in Thane's office at Millside Police Station.

Moss sat opposite him, once more going over the scrawled writing on the pad before him.

'We've got the paint scrapes. We've got the fact that Renfield was on a day off and out in his car on Thursday afternoon. We found this disturbed earth on the floor of his lock-up, the fact that he's been spending a fair amount of money. His girl says he had a wad of notes on Friday night.

'Then Mrs Senior, his landlady, says he has seemed a bit strange lately. His car's been found parked—call it abandoned —in a side street where nobody has ever seen it before. And, most important of all, Wheeler now identifies his photograph.'

Thane nodded wearily. 'You forgot one thing, Phil. That bus ticket. You know, I've got the craziest idea that that ticket, that piece of paper which gave us our first lead, could easily be my own. I told you he sometimes gave me lifts in the morning. It could have dropped out of my pocket when I took out a handkerchief, cigarettes, anything like that. He's our man all right. But I wonder if a jury would find him guilty on the sort of circumstantial evidence that we've got.'

'The chauffeur and cashier may identify him,' protested Moss.

'As what? Resembling the height and build of a murderer? You know what a jury's like on a murder case. Scared stiff they'll convict the wrong man. Remember the old legal formula—any possible doubt belongs to the accused. It is not for the defence to prove their man innocent. It is for the Crown to prove him guilty. Just imagine what a smart defence Q.C. could do to our friend Wheeler—the man who didn't know a killer the day after he saw him pass. The man who couldn't identify Renfield in the flesh, but picked another suspect instead—and only realised his error when he saw a photograph. Poor little Wheeler wouldn't know whether he was coming or going after the sort of cross-examination he could be put through, and neither would the jury.

'We need more evidence than we have before we take him to court. And right now we haven't even got Renfield. Let's see now. The Irish boats are covered?'

'Glasgow and Stranraer,' confirmed Moss.

The whole routine of search was in operation. Throughout Britain, at ports, aerodromes, bus and railway stations, police, alerted by radio and teleprinter messages, were quietly watching for anyone answering the reporter's description. Traffic out of Glasgow was being stopped and examined on every main road.

The men whose job it was, knew that the man they sought was almost definitely the killer who had already shot one of their comrades and who might well shoot again. Polite, civil, giving no indication of the reason for their vigil, they could not relax for a moment, despite the seemingly never-ending streams of innocent, protesting travellers whom they had to stop, scrutinise, then wave on.

'Wonder why he did it, Colin,' mused Moss. 'Think it was the girl?'

'Certain of it. She's a hot little number, out for what she can get, I'd say. I can imagine her going to the young fool's head. You know, I feel almost sorry for him. Funny, isn't it? He murders Macrae, and yet I can still have some sympathy left. Renfield's gone bad all right, probably really bad by now. Yet if it had been some other girl he would probably never have drifted off the straight.'

There was a knock on the door, and a detective constable entered. 'Another stolen car, sir,' he reported. 'A Rover this time. I don't think it's of much use, though. It was taken from a garage in Partick, and the thief helped himself to some spotlights from the accessories display on the way out.'

'Thanks, Lochran,' said Thane. 'That's the fourth tonight, isn't it? If he has stolen a car, I think the best bets are either that Hillman from outside the church or the Ford from the Sunday cinema car park.

'See if you can get us some coffee, son, will you? And better get some sandwiches, too. By the way, make sure that that photograph of Renfield we're having copied comes over from Headquarters the moment it is ready, and that prints go to every division. Headquarters will take care of the copies for the other forces, but I'll look after the one for the Gazette myself.'

The Scottish Police Gazette was the private bulletin circulated from Glasgow to police offices throughout the country. It contained details of men wanted, property stolen, information sought, and amounted to a daily report on the battle against crime.

Thane grimaced at his inspector as the youngster went out. 'Not much more we can do except wait. After this cuppa I think I'll try to catch some sleep.'

They were just finishing the last of the pot of coffee, however, when Lochran once more returned, this time with definite news.

'The Hillman's been found, sir, at Larbert. And another car's been stolen there.'

He handed Thane the message sheet torn from the tele printer, and Moss moved quickly round the desk to read the message over his chief's shoulder.

Stirling County H.Q. to Glasgow, urgent attention Thane, Millside. Hillman Minx reported stolen Glasgow found Larbert. Triumph T.R.2 Sports reported stolen Larbert. Man answering description Renfield seen walking in main street, direction park from which Triumph taken.

The message went on to give details of the Triumph and explain that the beat man had twice passed the parked Hillman before the special search message and Renfield's description had been passed to him by his sergeant.

'Swapping cars,' exclaimed Thane. 'Now where is he heading for? Larbert... that's on the way to Kincardine Bridge. Or he could be swinging through Stirling.

'He's heading home, Colin,' declared Moss. Renfield comes from Dundee. He's heading north. Maybe he's got some pal he hopes will get him aboard a ship there. He must be wriggling along the side roads. Remember, this boy knows all the ropes when it comes to a police hunt. He won't stick to the main highways.'

'Get an acknowledgement out, Phil,' instructed Thane. 'And pass on that suggestion to the Dundee force and the counties round about. I'm going to get my head down or a nap. But tell them downstairs to wake me immediately they get any word. You'd better get some sleep, too. We may have a lot of travelling ahead of us before morning.'

Despite the power and speed of the loo-mile-an-hour car under his control, David Renfield made slow progress on the twisting cross-country path he was taking towards Prestwick Airport. If he had headed there direct from Glasgow, it would have been a distance of only about thirty miles. But heading for Larbert, he added twenty-one miles to that distance, and now, on the byways route he was following, the mileage was nearer eighty, much of it on narrow, twisting roads where speeds in excess of forty were seldom practicable.

Near the halfway mark in his journey, with the lights of Strathaven glimmering in the distance, Renfield had to travel for a short distance down a main road. Suddenly, less than a mile ahead, he saw the red rear lights of a number of stopped cars, the white pinpricks of torches around the leaders.

'Police roadblock,' he cursed. But luck was riding with the Triumph. A small side road appeared ahead and he swung the little two-seater into it, on a wide curve past the search party.

At last, at nearly midnight, the car topped a little hill and Renfield saw in the distance the long streamer of lights which marked the main runways at Prestwick.

A plane was coming in, a giant airliner from across the Atlantic, he guessed, as its droning bulk passed between him and the cloud-fringed moon.

Fumbling in the dark pool of the passenger seat, his fingers once more found and felt the shape of the money-filled haversack. Renfield had come this distance in no wild hope of stowing away on an airliner.

Passports, customs, bookings... there was no hope in that direction with the police watch in progress. The Americans on the large United States Air Force base attached to the airport were free and easy. But whatever the truth of wartime stories of pilots' friends being whisked across the ocean for weekends in the sparkle of New York, that day was over.

There remained Bill Grosvenor. Bill, a Canadian, had been an Air Transport Auxiliary pilot during World War Two, flying lease-lend aircraft to Britain from North America for a thousand pounds a month when Prestwick was still sprouting from a few grass fields to one of the main strategic air strips in the free world.

Now, happily settled with his Scots wife, Bill lived near the airport and had a second-hand American plane, a Cessna, which he ran as a charter service, a literal aerial taxi. The Cessna, a single-engine four-seater, with a top speed of 140 m.p.h., was an ideal business aircraft. The Evening View was one of Grosvenor's regular newspaper customers, and between various hire jobs of one kind and another Bill made quite a little bit of money. He spent the rest of his time helping his wife run the small tourist gift shop which was their other interest.

The Triumph bumped and swayed as it was turned off the road and across a patch of rough grassland. Renfield halted it behind a line of bushes. Back down the road a little lay a scattered little collection of cottages, all now darkened. In the middle of them was a brightly lit telephone box.

Renfield picked up his haversack from the car seat, opened the door, and made to leave the two-seater. With an irritated snap of his fingers, he turned back and switched off the sidelights. He didn't want the Triumph found till morning, and some passing Nosey Parker might investigate the glimmer from its bulbs.

It took nearly ten minutes of cautious walking—one hand clutching the old gas mask cover, the other tight round the butt of the automatic, hidden in his coat pocket—before he reached the phone box. The fields around seemed alive with rustling, unseen shapes. The sudden chilling scream of a young rabbit as a weasel struck it down clashed on his jangled nerves.

Finally he was inside the telephone box, searching in the directory. G—Grass—Gro—Grosvenor, W. Prestwick 6124. He had no coppers left. "Only pound notes," he laughed slightly hysterically to himself. Renfield dialled "0."

When the operator's sleepy voice answered, he offered a shilling for the call, explaining that he had no change.

'Right,' said the man's voice, as the coin made two tinkling clicks going into the box. 'Don't press button A till your number...'

The coin clattered further down the mechanism as Renfield deliberately pressed. 'Sorry,' he apologised.

'I don't mind, Mac,' yawned the operator. 'It's your funeral if there's no reply.'

There was a reply. And Renfield, no tell-tale "click" to reveal he was in a local call box, launched into his tale.

Grosvenor had answered the telephone almost immediately. He had been making a last round of the house before going to bed when the bell had begun sounding. As his drawling voice came over the wire, the reporter told him, 'Renfield of the View here, Mr Grosvenor. We've got a little job for that plane of yours, if it is available.

'Always ready to help you boys—for money,' cracked Grosvenor. 'Why, where, and how soon you planning on going?'

'Stornoway, in about two hours,' he replied. 'We've had a

rush message that a Fleetwood trawler is coming in there with five injured aboard after an outbreak of fire at sea. I'm coming down to Prestwick almost right away—if you can do the job, that is?'

'Uh-uh, can't be done as soon as that,' protested Grosvenor. 'Stornoway Airport will be closed by now, and I can't risk an unassisted night landing up there. Now, if you can wait so that we get over it by dawn... that'd mean leaving at say about 4.30 a.m.

'There's a regular air service to Stornoway from Renfrew Airport, you know. That's just beside Glasgow—and cheaper. Why drag me in?'

'This is a hurry-up job,' explained Renfield. 'We'll want to send pictures back. If that's the earliest you can manage, it will just have to do. Oh, how about the airport authorities?'

He crossed his fingers tightly as he waited.

'Not to worry,' replied the Canadian. 'For a local trip like this, all I do is file a flight plan a few minutes before take-off and pick up a weather report. I've got radio in the plane, so there's no other red tape.'

Renfield thought quickly. 'Fine, Mr Grosvenor. Look, keep this story angle strictly to yourself, will you? The View seems to have it to itself for the moment. The opposition papers will get on to it sooner or later, but as far as we are concerned the later the better. If it suits, I'll meet you at the car park near the aircraft hangars. It's quieter there than at the hotel.'

'See you then at four-thirty,' confirmed Grosvenor. 'Now I'm off to get some shut-eye. I'll need it if I'm going to drive this plane for you.'

He hung up.

Breathing a sigh of relief that the Canadian had not noticed the absence of time "pips" normally present on a long-distance call, Renfield replaced the receiver. He opened the telephone box door, and, after a glance up and down the silent street, began walking back the way he had come.

His big gamble had begun, the stake, his freedom. If he managed to get into the air with Grosvenor that plane wasn't flying to Stornoway. The pilot would be persuaded at gunpoint, plus an offer of five hundred pounds, to land somewhere in Holland.

Grosvenor would be a man with a lot to lose if he refused, and plenty to gain for a comparatively small service. "If only Thane doesn't catch on," Renfield muttered as he continued down the road. "He is certain to have a watch on the regular passenger routes. But he won't be concerned with other local flights—I hope. He hasn't had time. He probably hasn't got enough on me yet to take really drastic action."

For a moment he contemplated sitting in the car until nearer the time when he was to meet the airman. He decided against it, however, and instead sat down beneath one of the nearby bushes, the precious money at his side, the automatic on his lap. It was simply a matter of staying awake. And the wet ground, the chill breeze, and, above all, the immensity of the coming gamble, constituted no lullaby.

CHAPTER TWENTY-NINE

BILL GROSVENOR WAS A METHODICAL MAN. At half-past two in the morning, after only a brief rest, he went downstairs to the kitchen of his home, set the coffee percolator going, then went to the telephone and dialled a Prestwick Airport number, one which would connect him direct with the Ministry of Civil Aviation's Met Office, where weather information from over a vast area was constantly on tap.

'That you, Tony?' he asked. 'Grosvenor here. I've got to make a little hop up to Stornoway in about a couple of hours. I'll be picking up the forecast sheet later—but be a pal and give me a rough idea just now, will you?'

Tony agreed. There was silence for a few minutes, then the Met man returned to the phone.

'Not very happy-making, Bill,' he warned. 'Here's the flight forecast along the route for 3,000 feet. Wind 250 degrees, 20 knots, cloudy conditions with possibly some rain or drizzle. Visibility say two to four miles. Six-eighths to eight-eighths of strato cumulus and stratus.'

'That means wet, windy and cloudy, I suppose. Still, I can

manage that. What are the landing conditions like at Stornoway?'

'Bad. Surface wind southwest, eight knots, visibility one mile. Eight-eighths stratus cloud as low as one hundred feet. Comes under the heading of hazardous.'

Grosvenor moaned in disgust. 'Too much for this boy, I'm afraid. Thanks, Tony. You've saved me a lot of worry.'

Renfield waited. In Glasgow, Thane dozed on his camp bed, shoes and jacket off, but otherwise fully dressed.

And then, at 3 a.m., the telephone rang in the hallway of Mrs Senior's home. One of the two policemen who were remaining on guard at the landlady's house answered it, giving only the instrument's number.

'Is that Mr Renfield?' queried the voice on the other end. 'This is Bill Grosvenor calling.'

'No, this isn't Mr Renfield,' replied the policeman. 'Who's speaking again? Can I give him a message?'

'Yeah. Look, Renfield's paper wants me to fly him to Stornoway this morning. My name's Grosvenor. I've got a charter plane at Prestwick Airport. I tried his office, but there's only a couple of morning paper men left there, and they know nothing about the flight. The telephone operator at the *View* gave me this number and told me to ring Renfield at home. He hasn't left yet, has he?'

The constable, excited now, waved frantically to his sleepy-eyed colleague. 'This is the police, Mr Grosvenor. We are very anxious to get in touch with Renfield. Tell me about this flight in your plane, will you?'

The other policeman shoved an open notebook and pencil

on the little table beside the phone, and the man at the receiver began to scribble furiously.

'Oh.' Grosvenor was silent for a moment as he digested this somewhat startling news. 'Is something up? Say, what I wanted to tell him anyway is that I can't make the trip. I've just checked on the phone with the met. office at the airport. Conditions over Stornoway are, to put it mildly, ruddy awful. I couldn't risk trying a landing. Tell me, friend, what have the police got to do with this anyway?'

'I'm afraid we can't divulge that just now,' the policeman carefully replied. 'Where are you speaking from? And what time was the flight to have been at?'

'My home in Prestwick, and we were to have met at four-thirty. Say, you aren't pulling my leg or something?

'Definitely not. Now, if you'll give me your telephone number, you'll be called back in a very few minutes. And, look sir, this is very important. Don't leave your home, and if Renfield contacts you again, don't tell him anything. Just act as if you are going to meet him as arranged.

The Canadian, still puzzled, more than a little worried, agreed. He had hardly replaced his receiver before the policeman was dialling Millside Police Station and asking for Chief Inspector Thane.

Colin Thane was only half asleep when the phone tinkled. He answered within seconds, and a look of triumph came on his face as the man told of Grosvenor's call.

'Good show! You played it perfectly. What's Grosvenor's telephone number? Right, now hang up, I've got work to do.'

Almost dancing with excitement, he wakened Moss.

'We've got him, Phil. He's trying to get out of Prestwick on a small charter plane in just over an hour. Told some cock and bull story to the pilot. We'll need to move fast.'

Waiting only to pad on stocking soles back to his room and

pull on his shoes and jacket, he hurried along to the C.I.D. duty room, where the night duty officers were quietly waiting.

'Edwards, get on the blower and have a fast car stand by with driver. Corrie, phone this number and get hold of a man called Grosvenor. Tell him that I'm on my way down, and not to move till I get there. Then contact Prestwick police, let them know that Renfield's around the airport, but ask them not to do anything except have some men standing by. Oh—see if they can get a plain clothes man round to Grosvenor's house without too much of a fuss.'

Moss, hurriedly fastening his tie, entered the room. 'We going down there, Colin?' Then, 'He's got a gun. Do you think...?' He left the question unspoken.

Thane hesitated. Revolvers were kept at the police station. They were there only as a last resort, left untouched, apart from cleaning, from one year to another by men who took pride in the tradition that Britain's police went unarmed.

'Maybe we'd better. One each—I'll sign the book. But they're strictly for insurance,' he decided.

Moss unlocked the safe and brought out two .38 calibre revolvers, laying a box of cartridges beside them on the nearest desk. Then he went for his coat.

It is thirty miles from Glasgow to Prestwick, part of it over one of the best roads in Britain. The police car, a light blue Jaguar, covered the distance in seconds under thirty minutes, a roaring, wind-buffeted run, with the faintly-lit speedometer needle hovering around the 95 mark in the long four-lane straights and dropping just below the 65 point on the few curving corners. Every now and again its racing wheels, running across the lines of "cat's eye" road markers, sent a quick "thrump-thrump-thrump" rippling and shivering through the car.

The Jaguar's siren cut in with a wail as they streaked

through Kilmarnock's long, narrow and empty main street—brake, double declutch into lower gear, tyres scream round the huge roundabout at the Cross, accelerate again, change gear—then they raced into the darkness again, as suddenly as if a cloak had been thrown across the road. Twelve miles to go!

Clinging to the dashboard while Moss sat tense behind him, Thane shut his eyes as the Jaguar, its police driver relaxed, hands at the "ten to two" position on the wheel, went into a "drift" to take the left-hand bend at the top of a long, winding hill and seemed headed straight for a pair of glaring headlights coming sizzling towards them.

The driver gave a quick double-flick to the wheel—and the car, amid a scream of rubber, "shimmied" and miraculously appeared set on its own side of the road, while the other vehicle, an airline bus carrying passengers from Prestwick to Glasgow, whipped past.

'God Almighty!' choked Moss. 'My guts weren't built for this sort of thing. I don't feel so good.'

'Not long now, sir,' said the driver, a grin flickering on his lips in the darkness. Upsetting senior officers and obeying orders at the same time was a rather unusual lot, but quite an interesting one.

On they roared, round another corner, over a rise. Then the airport's identity beacon light streaked across the sky... and again, brighter, nearer. The car slowed for the last corner before the airport, and got underway again. Seconds later, with a suddenness which almost shot Thane through the window and Moss over into the front seat, the driver clamped on the brakes.

A white-coated figure was waving a red lamp in the middle of the road, while to his right the airport flarepath was ablaze with coloured lights.

'What the hell's going on?' queried Moss, gathering

himself up and nursing a banged shin, while Thane pushed himself back on the seat. 'What's that character up to?'

'Plane coming in, sir,' explained the driver. 'Here it comes.'

With a roar which pounded against their eardrums and seemed to fill and shake the car, the airliner, lights winking like the decorations on a Christmas tree, passed before them only a few feet off the ground. Hardly had it crossed their path than the white-coated figure—an airport policeman—waved them on down the road, which formed a metalled ribbon cutting across the grass-covered approach to the main runway.

As the car moved off, the two detectives caught a glimpse of the plane, now touched down, taxiing swiftly along the lane of lights, its long journey over.

Halting only at the town centre, about a mile on, to ask the way to the house from a patrolling policeman, they reached their destination within a few minutes. Lights burned in the ground-floor windows of the smart stone villa. Their ring at the doorbell was answered by Grosvenor, who had obviously been anxiously awaiting them.

Fully dressed, a silk scarf tucked into the open neck of his shirt, the Canadian was puffing a cigar which Moss, after one agonised sniff, stayed well away from.

'You Chief Detective Inspector Thane? Say, you certainly didn't waste any time coming down. Now can you tell me what this crazy set-up is all about?'

Thane answered with a question. 'Any more word from Renfield?'

Grosvenor shook his head, and led them into the lounge of his home, where a local police sergeant, in plain clothes, was already waiting.

Thane spoke quickly. 'Mr Grosvenor, I can't tell you everything. There isn't time. But you may have read of the payroll hold-up in Glasgow last Thursday afternoon, in which a policeman was shot and killed. We have reason to believe that this man Renfield was the masked motorcyclist who committed the crime, and that he may be armed. He is suspected of stealing two cars tonight, and is almost certainly using your plane to make a getaway.'

The Canadian gave a long low whistle. Then he queried, 'But say, Mr Thane, why would he want to go to a dump like Stornoway?'

Thane gazed steadily at the stockily built pilot.

'I believe, Mr Grosvenor, that once in the air you might be —let's say asked to change your destination. The man must be prepared to risk everything, on your plane being his means of escape. He laid a false trail north from Glasgow, which made us think that he was heading for the north-east ports, trying to get on a ship.

'We would be concentrating our search up there still if you had not made that telephone call. Of course, you'll understand from what I've told you that Renfield's newspaper knows nothing about this proposed trip.'

The Canadian chewed at his cigar. 'Looks like the first time I've ever had cause to bless the fact that the weather is stopping me from flying. I hate to think of being up there alone with a guy like that. You'll go and pick him up now, I suppose?'

'I'm afraid it isn't just as simple as that. I presume Renfield knows you by sight?'

'Sure. I've taken him up a few times, usually with a photographer. The last time was for a trip over a wrecked ship. Why?'

'Renfield will be waiting for you, and you alone, to arrive. If he is the man we believe him to be, then he won't hesitate to shoot if he finds himself trapped and has a chance to act. We want to avoid that at all costs.

'Exactly where have you arranged to meet him? I don't suppose he chose the actual passenger terminal building?

'No, not there. Here, I'll show you...' The Canadian picked up a couple of small brass ornaments from the mantelpiece and placed them a short distance apart on the nearby coffee-table.

Drawing a finger along the table between them, he explained, 'Take this line I'm drawing as the main runway. This ornament on the one side is the airport hotel—the terminal. The other ornament, on the other side of the runway and a good bit further away from the main road, is the maintenance area car park. I've to meet him, he arranged, about there. The twister told me that it would be quieter, and that he didn't want people to know anything about his "story."'

'From what you say it should be quiet enough,' agreed Thane. 'But there must be no possibility of his breaking loose and somehow managing to run amok. He might even get across to the airport buildings. Women and children are among the passengers who will be there, and bullets take no account of sex or age. We dare not take risks.'

Grosvenor, eyes narrowing, perched himself on the arm of the couch, took another puff at his cigar, and asked, 'So?'

'So I want to ask you to behave as if the weather was fine and you suspected nothing. I want you to drive down alone to meet him. And then, when you are together and nearly at the plane, his guard should come down a bit. That's when we'll jump him.

'We're dealing with a dangerous, armed man, who'll be fighting for his freedom. There's always the chance that something might go wrong.

'It is your decision. What do you say?'

CHAPTER THIRTY

GROSVENOR BLEW A LONG, thick cloud of cigar smoke slowly through his lips, hesitated, then asked, 'How about telling me what you've got in mind first? And, I don't know about you, but I'm going to have a drink. I think better with a glass in my hand.'

He went over to the sideboard, opened it, and asked, 'Like a whisky, Mr Thane?'

'Not for me, thanks,' replied the detective. 'My friends might, though. We'll say they're off duty for the next couple of minutes.'

Moss and the sergeant expressed their thanks, and Grosvenor filled the three glasses and passed two of them across.

'Can we sit down?'

Thane settled himself in a chair, as did the pilot, glass in hand, while Moss and the sergeant occupied the couch.

'We've got about twenty minutes left before you are due to meet Renfield. My plan, frankly, is completely based on using you as bait. Renfield is a highly intelligent opponent. Every last detail about the hold-up shows that. Oh, we could throw a cordon round the car park, all right. But even if he didn't see us moving in and slip through unseen, he would certainly become suspicious when you didn't turn up. And he might try to shoot his way out. Some of our men would be certain to be hurt, and he would stand a fair chance of getting away.'

'So you are asking me to be the cheese in the police mouse-trap,' murmured Grosvenor, drumming his fingers on the arm of his chair and sipping his drink.

'It's the only way. If you'll do it—and it's only fair to warn you again that this is a dangerous task, and one that is your decision entirely either to say yes or no—I want you to go along to the car park alone. You've got a car?'

'A '53 Studebaker,' confirmed the Canadian.

'Well, I want you to drive there, meet Renfield just as arranged, pretend everything is normal as far as you are concerned, and walk over towards your plane with him. Keep him talking, about anything. Is there anywhere near the plane where two or three men could hide?'

'Just at the side of the hangar.'

'Right, we'll wait there. Beside the plane is probably about the last place he'll expect trouble. And that's where we'll take him.

'Now it's up to you. Are you prepared to take the chance?'

The Canadian sat silent, the fingers of his left hand still drumming on the armchair.

Then, with a nervous smile, he rose, emptying his whisky glass at a gulp. 'Guess we haven't much time left, Inspector. Let's get organised.'

'You'll do it! Good man!'

Thane turned towards the local police sergeant, sitting nursing his empty glass over on the couch.

'Sergeant, I wonder if, while Mr Grosvenor is getting

ready, you would find out from him the best way of getting to where his plane lies without our being seen from the car park. You know the area, so you will be able to follow his directions better than either of us could. Meantime, I'd like to use your phone, if I may, Mr Grosvenor?'

'Help yourself,' grunted the pilot. 'It's over in the corner of the room. I've let you talk me into being a king-sized bait. Guess I might as well go the whole hog and give you the freedom of the telephone. Say, my wife's upstairs, wide awake. I had to practically hog-tie her to stop her coming downstairs to find out what the heck's going on. I'll spin her a yarn that the police want me to take you on a short flight. She knows there's a trip in the wind, but nothing of the details.

'I don't want her to get to know what I'm doing. She worries enough every time I go flying without hearing I'm setting up as a spare-time unpaid cop.'

'Certainly, sir. Only we haven't much time,' reminded Moss.

Thane was already on the telephone to Prestwick Police Station, where he found a helpful inspector in charge.

Quickly running over the developments that had taken place, the Glasgow man asked for two car-loads of police to wait near the airport gates, ready to drive in towards the car park and hangars as soon as they heard a whistle blast.

'Could you also get in touch with the airport authorities, and warn them about what is going on? I'd like the airport police on duty at the gate leading to that part of the aerodrome told to allow absolutely no traffic in, except the police and Grosvenor's car.

'Will they know his car? Yes, it's the Studebaker. Good. And tell them to do nothing else, absolutely nothing. We're doing it this way to try to avoid any chance of casualties.'

He hung up. A couple of minutes later Grosvenor and the policemen parted on the steps of the house.

Joining Thane and Moss in the Jaguar, the Ayrshire sergeant, who had been quickly briefed by the Canadian, guided the driver on a route which would take them round the outer limits of the aerodrome. It led to a side road which ran fairly close to the hangar in which lay the light plane.

'We'll have to climb a fence, sir,' he warned. It's barbed wire, I'm afraid, but for our purpose it's the safest place to try.'

The Jaguar swept back through the sleeping town, past the airport, and turned up first one road, then another.

'Now,' said the sergeant, tapping the driver on the shoulder, and the man obediently switched off both engine and lights and allowed the car to coast slowly and silently to a halt. The car's radio was useless, being on a different frequency from that used by the Ayrshire force. Thane could only trust that the rest of his plan was working smoothly.

'Go on up the road a bit, then turn round and head back to the airport entrance,' he told the driver. You'll find a couple of local cars there. Stay with them.'

The Jaguar slid away, its engine a mere purr. Still without lights, it faded into the darkness, while Thane and Moss followed the sergeant over to the fence. They struggled over its strands, Moss swearing softly as a barb caught his trouser leg close to the turn-up and tore a fragment of cloth.

Then they were in the airport. Guided by the local man, they moved cautiously over the fairly even ground until they reached tarmac, then slipped quietly across into the deeper shadow of a large brick building.

Walking quietly, they wore their way along its side and past two smaller sheds. A faint shimmer coming from its polished metal wings in the almost imperceptible moonlight, an aircraft loomed ahead in the darkness.

'This it?' whispered Thane.

The sergeant shook his head.

'Next hangar—another three hundred yards,' came his equally quiet reply.

This time there was no sign of a building to give them cover. The distance was completely across open tarmac. The trio waited until a particularly thick cloud damped down the moon-glow to almost nil, then, moving quickly and silently, sped across the ground.

They reached the back of the building, a huge metal shell, and, breathing heavily, slipped forward once more, halting just at the corner before the open front of the hangar.

'Looks like we're in time all right,' murmured Moss. 'No sign of them approaching yet. What now, Colin?'

'We wait just here, out of sight,' replied Thane. 'We'll jump Renfield just as he enters the hangar. Keep your gun handy, but remember, we won't use them except as a last resort.'

The three men stood pressed against the cold metal wall, silent, tensed.

CHAPTER THIRTY-ONE

DAVID RENFIELD WAS ALSO WAITING. About an hour before, he had left the little patch of bushes where he had sheltered and, cold and shivering, had begun to walk down the road towards the airport.

Twice the sound of an engine warned him of an approaching car, and he had had to throw himself into the nearest cover until the vehicle's headlights had swept past. But finally, he was able to clamber over an iron gate guarding an old entrance to the airport and set about finding his way to the car park.

By night, however, the aerodrome was like an uncharted jungle. All the little day-time landmarks disappeared and instead a confusion of lights of all shapes and colours glittered everywhere.

Frantically seeking his bearings, he walked on until he almost blundered into a small stream which flowed a short distance away from the main runway.

"For heaven's sake take your time," he told himself. "Let's try and make some sense out of these lights. That must be the runway over there. Yes, there's the control tower down towards the far end on the other side. That means the car park should be somewhere down on the right here."

Shoes squelching in the mud, he cut across the grass towards his goal. His feet tripped over a wire at one point, a rubber-covered cable snaking along the ground towards, he guessed, some lighting installation. The haversack flew from his hand as he fell to his knees, and for a moment he crawled blindly in the darkness to recover it.

Checking the safety catch on his automatic, he went forward slowly until the faint outline of the huge Scottish Aviation building loomed ahead and he recognised the car park lying a little way from it. There were only a few cars in the park, one normally used solely by airport personnel. The group of buildings scattered around seemed deserted.

Leaving the grass, Renfield walked the two hundred yards across the tarmac surface to where the line of vehicles stood silent and empty. Gun in hand, every moment he expected a hail, a challenge, a beam of light to cut the darkness and pin him down. But nothing happened.

"Made it," he triumphed. "The police can't possibly know I'm here. Grosvenor will be along in a few minutes, we take off... and then the Continent's next stop."

He sat down on the running-board of one of the cars a waited, ears strained for the slightest sound.

Bill Grosvenor had never been so scared in all his chequered life as he was when he got his Studebaker out of the garage and drove away from home.

He gave a wave out of the car window to the darkened upstairs bedroom of his home, where he knew his wife was watching, as she always did when he left for an early morning flight.

"Oh baby, if only you knew what's going on," he thought to himself. "This boy would rather be anywhere right now, than in the jam I've landed myself in."

He grated the car down a gear as he approached the road. All these plans explained by the Glasgow cop appeared to dovetail nicely when he had heard them in the warm comfort of his home.

But now, alone in the car, driving to his appointment with a man with a gun who was desperate, who had killed once already, Grosvenor wished himself a hundred miles away from the airport.

Down the main road, past the first entrance to the airport, then the second, he drove. His fingers quivered as he flipped over the trafficator switch, making the signal lights blink their fore-and-aft warning that he was about to turn.

A dark blue uniformed airport policeman stood in the middle of the entrance road, handheld upwards in an unmistakable command. Grosvenor slowed, stopped, and the man came round to the driver's door.

As the pilot wound down the window, the airport man peered in at him. He nodded recognition, whispered, 'Good luck, chum,' and stepped back.

Not even on his long, dangerous trans-Atlantic flights had the Canadian felt so alone. He set off once more, the Studebaker travelling at a snail's pace up the road towards the parking ground.

Backing the Studebaker into position beside the other cars, he reluctantly switched off the motor, doused the lights and stepped out.

Then, as if it had materialised from nowhere, he saw the figure walking towards him. He wanted to run. But Renfield spoke, and the Canadian realised once and for all that it was too late to back out.

'Morning, Mr Grosvenor,' the reporter greeted him cheerily. 'Hell of an early hour to drag you out. Everything all set?'

'Yes,' agreed the pilot, then, playing his part, 'The Cessna's all gassed up, and I've booked the flight plan O.K. The weather isn't too hot, but we'll make it all right.'

'Fair enough,' replied the reporter. 'If you want, lock your car, and we'll just get moving. Mine is lying back there,' he added, gesturing vaguely along the line of vehicles. 'Er—I hope you kept the reason for the trip to yourself and the fact that you were taking me as a passenger?'

'Sure, sure,' blurted the pilot. 'I didn't tell a soul, so help me.' He fumbled with the key at the car door, while Renfield stood by impatiently. Finally, it turned in the lock. He forced a grin to his face. 'Sure dark tonight. These clouds are getting thicker all the time. Getting so you'd hardly know there was a moon up there.'

Moving away from the car, he explained, 'We'll need to walk from here. It isn't too far, though. I've got a torch.'

'Don't trouble,' assured Renfield. 'My eyes are used to the darkness. I got down a bit early and just hung about waiting on you.'

They walked on in silence. Then Grosvenor asked, What's happening in Glasgow these days?' More daringly, he continued, 'Have they arrested anybody for that payroll robbery yet—what do they call the guy, Mr False Face?'

There was a noise like a chuckle from his companion. 'No, they haven't got anyone yet, and I don't think they ever will. The man who did that job was a very smart operator. He left nothing to chance. Nothing.'

Grosvenor, feeling that the best line of defence against

suspicion was to continue this vein of talk, asked, 'Didn't I see your name on a View story about the case?'

'Glad you noticed,' replied the reporter, still walking briskly. 'I was on the "False Face" job, but the news editor pulled me off it to go on this trawler story. It's a bit of a blow having to fall out of bed and get down here at this hour of the morning, but then, that's the sort of thing that happens in our business, and we just get used to it.

'How much further have we got to go, Mr Grosvenor? I didn't think it was as far as this.'

Grosvenor, who had already lengthened the route making two diversions in case Thane and his companion needed the extra time, shook his head.

'Probably the plane was out in the open the last time. Can you see that big building just on ahead? That's the hangar,' he explained. 'The plane's inside. There's no door on that hangar, one of the reasons why I can rent it pretty cheaply. As I said, the Cessna's all set,' he added in a rush of words. 'We'll be on our way within a couple of minutes.'

It was Moss who was the first of the three in hiding to spot the two approaching figures, their bodies showing for an instant as they were silhouetted against a distant haze of light which marked the airport terminal.

He whispered the news to Thane and the sergeant. The big Ayrshire policeman pulled his soft hat a little tighter on his forehead, brought a wooden baton out from beneath his overcoat, and spat quietly on the polished tip.

'For luck,' he grinned. Thane allowed a smile to cross his face, then, slowly, reluctantly, pulled the pistol from his pocket. Moss already had his in his hand.

Renfield and the pilot were so close that they could hear their footsteps and a murmur of conversation.

And then it happened. A powerful white beam of light suddenly lanced out to bathe the side of the hangar, and a stentorian American voice bellowed, 'Hey, what do you guys think you're up to? Stay right where you are.'

Thane spun round with an oath, but could see nothing for the blinding light.

'Hey, Maxie,' came a second American accent. 'Watch it. They got guns!'

'Holy cow!' exclaimed the first voice. The light flicked out —at the same instant as the sound of a scuffle, a cry, and the clatter of running feet came from where Grosvenor and Renfield had been.

Thane ran out from the shelter of the hangar wall, blowing shrill blasts on his whistle. 'We're police, you fools,' bellowed Moss in the direction of the American voices, then turned to follow. The big sergeant was already galloping into the darkness after Thane.

The torch flickered on again as its owner and his companion sprinted over. Thane, bending over a groaning Bill Grosvenor who was lying in a twisted position on the ground, found himself the focus of the little group. The two police cars which had been waiting outside could be heard roaring towards the scene.

Gently the two detectives turned the pilot over, and Moss put an arm round the Canadian's back, raising his head. A savage, broken weal of skin and blood lay at an angle across Grosvenor's forehead.

'It's Thane, Grosvenor,' the Chief Inspector said, his lips close to the injured man's ear. 'What happened?'

'That guy...' the Canadian mumbled. 'He slammed me across the head with a gun. That light... gave the game away.

He's got a haversack with him. Guess that's where... where the money is. Watch him. Vicious.' He groaned again, shutting his eyes in pain.

Thane rose to his feet. 'That wallop may have fractured his skull. We'll need to get him to hospital. What in God's name happened back there?'

'Guess it's our fault, mister,' said one of the two men who had upset the plan, a small, thin figure in the uniform of a U.S. Air Force corporal. 'Me and my buddy were taking a shortcut from our part of the airfield down towards the airport building to relieve a couple of our boys. We saw you hiding there. You might have been prowlers, or even Commies out to sabotage our jets for all we knew.

'Say, who's the guy that got away? Was he important? You gave us one hell of a scare when we saw these guns.'

'Maxie, something tells me these cops are angry,' said the second American. 'Look, if we can help...'

Thane was almost speechless with rage. 'You two half-wits have let a murderer get away,' he choked. 'My God, I'll have you tucked away in the worst cell in the worst jail in the whole of America for this.'

He broke off as the first of the two police cars, headlights blazing, halted beside the group. The occupants rushed over to him as the second car slowed, its doors opening. A third car, Thane's Jaguar, was driving up behind.

Momentarily ignoring the two crestfallen American airmen, he quickly explained what had happened in bitter tones to the newcomers. The sergeant, baton still in hand, returned from the darkness and entered the headlamp-bathed scene, shaking his head. Their quarry had disappeared, lost in the confusing darkness.

Two constables helped Grosvenor, still dazed and barely coherent, into the back of the Jaguar.

'Phil, you go with him,' ordered Thane. 'Take him to the airport terminal and see what can be done for him there. I'll radio for an ambulance to meet you. Then alert the airport police and get every man you can scrape together to seal all roads leading from the place.'

'How about you?' queried Moss. 'Can't I help here?'

'No. I'll just tidy up here and join you. There isn't much more we can do for the moment.'

The Jaguar drove off, and, while the newly arrived policemen, batons drawn, searched the immediate neighbourhood of the hangar in the faint hope that Renfield was still lurking nearby, Thane called up the Ayrshire police control on one of the local car's radio.

Arrangements were made for more police to be rushed to the airport, including some from neighbouring towns, and for cars to patrol all the roads around it. Thane had just replaced the microphone in the car when the American corporal approached him once more.

'Look, sir, we're helluva sorry. My name's Valleni—Corporal Max Valleni. Can't we help? Me and a few of the boys could take a look around for you, kinda make up for the mess we made of things.'

The C.I.D. man looked at the small eager figure in the sky-blue uniform. He regretted the way in which he had flown off the handle at the two airmen, almost as much as he regretted the way their butting in had allowed Renfield to skip literally from his grasp.

'Thanks for the offer,' he answered. 'I'm sorry, too, that I lost my temper. If I had been in your shoes I would probably have done exactly what you did. But this is a police matter. We'll handle it.'

The American's embarrassed grin suddenly froze as, seconds after Thane had finished speaking, the sound of a shot rang out, having as its echo a cry of pain. They had come from somewhere to the left of the men.

'Hey, that's up among our jet fighters!' exclaimed Corporal Valleni. 'They're parked up about that way.'

'Show us!'

Thane bundled the American into the nearest police car, and the driver sent it racing over the tarmac in the direction indicated, while the other car, facing the opposite direction, hurriedly turned to follow, police scrambling aboard.

Above the noise of the engine they heard another heavier shot, and another. Then the headlights, swinging as the car swept round a bend in the metalled track, picked out a row of American jets and, a score or so yards in front of them, the figure of a man on his knees, one hand clutching his side, a gun in the other pointing into the darkness. Even as they approached, he fired again, towards an invisible target.

Valleni swore quietly. 'Whether you like it or not, mister, we've just joined your army. That's one of our night guards, and it looks as though he's met up with your buddy.'

As the police car stopped only a few yards from the injured man, the sound of a warning hooter was already piercing the air over in the American Air Force camp, a short distance away. Lights could be seen snapping on as the airmen, wakened from sleep, scrambled into their clothing and prepared to turn out.

Nearer at hand, whistles blew and shouts could be heard as other American sentries ran towards the spot.

For a second time in a few minutes Thane found himself bending over an injured man. The wounded airman, a brawny Private First Class, had been hit in the left side by a bullet. While the police driver stood guard, Thane and Corporal Valleni ripped open the man's tunic and shirt and tried to plug the wound, using their handkerchiefs in an attempt to stem the flowing blood.

'What happened, Charlie?' asked Valleni as they worked.

The wounded airman, ebony face contorted with pain, tried to rise to his feet and had to be forced to stay down while he told them, 'Some dirty son jes' came running out of the darkness towards me. I shouted to him to stop. He kinda slowed, and I raised my night-stick, jes' so he wouldn't try anything. I hadn't seen the gun he had in his hand. First I knew of it was when he fired at me.

'It jes' burned into me and knocked me over,' groaned the sentry. 'Then my revolver stuck in the goddam holster, and by the time I got it out he'd nipped back in there the way he had come.'

Out in the direction he pointed, towards the centre of the airport, the glowing web of runway lights suddenly switched on, tracing their pattern across the carpet-like surface of the ground. The sound of an airliner coming into land filled the sky.

'Did I get him, Corp.?' asked the wounded man.

'Maybe, Charlie, maybe,' soothed Valleni. 'Here's some of the boys coming. We'll find out.'

Half a dozen airmen carrying carbines and led by a staff sergeant came clattering towards the spot, slowing as they saw the stationary police car and the second car just drawing up behind it, loaded with more police.

'What goes on?' asked their leader. 'What were those shots?'

'Charlie here's been shot by some Britisher on the run,' replied Valleni. 'These cops were after him and—er—he got away. The guy's killed somebody already. Charlie shot at him, but doesn't know if he hit him.'

Thane broke in on the exchange. 'I'm a police officer,' he

hastily explained. 'The man we're after may be lying wounded out there somewhere. Could you help us take a look just around here? I'd better warn you he won't hesitate to kill.'

'We're with you, Mac!' exclaimed the staff sergeant. 'Hey, Louie. Get back to the camp and get that doggone ambulance up here, but quick. Tell the lieutenant what's going on. Joe, you stay with the corporal. The rest of us will help these cops.'

The two groups of men emerged, and, while the drivers of the two cars slowly moved their vehicles so that their headlight beams swept the area, they quickly quartered the area.

For fully ten minutes they searched. Then Thane, turning to the staff sergeant a few yards away from him, said, 'I think we'd better call it off. If he had been badly hurt he wouldn't have got as far as this. My problem now is to make sure he doesn't get off the airport.'

As they turned to go back, the C.I.D. man took one more look at the glittering airport. Somewhere amid all that manmade beauty Renfield was hiding, hunted, desperate, perhaps wounded.

Sleek, low-slung and heavily chromium-plated, the white-painted U.S.A.F. ambulance had arrived beside the wounded sentry, and the latter, protesting fiercely, was being forcefully ordered to 'lie down in the damned stretcher and quit arguing about it' by a medical orderly as the party returned from their fruitless search.

As they watched, the man, face a vivid contrast against the snow-white blanket placed over him, was quickly lifted through the rear doors. The two orderlies jumped in the back beside him, without bothering to shut the doors, and the ambulance growled back towards the camp.

'We've got a fully equipped hospital at the base,' explained the staff sergeant. 'Guys there will do anything from a manicure to a major carve-up. Say—I don't know your name. I'm Mick Haslett.'

'Chief Detective Inspector Thane, Glasgow Police,' introduced the detective.

'Glad to know you. Guess you'll want to meet our officer as soon as you can.' He bellowed, 'Hey, Lieutenant, over here!' and a man wearing American pilot's wings and officer insignia came towards them.

As soon as Lieutenant Bauer learned what had happened, he readily agreed to place as many men as he could find along the boundary of the American sector of the airport.

'We'll pen him in this side for you, Chief Inspector.' he promised. 'But what about the rest of the airport? It's a big place, you know.'

'I'm going back to the airport building right now,' said Thane. 'My inspector is down there trying to organise that sort of thing right now. And this shooting makes it more imperative than ever.'

The police car took only a few minutes to take the detective to the terminal building, where Moss was waiting. Twice on the way, however, it was stopped by patrolling police, concrete proof of the cordon that was being hurriedly thrown up.

Moss hurried towards his chief as soon as he entered the building. 'I heard about the shooting, Colin. This is getting pretty grim. There are more police on the way, and the airport people are helping. What do we do next?'

'Get that cordon as tight as possible, then get the top brass around here together and plan this search,' said Thane. 'You know, Phil, I don't think we're hunting an ordinary, thinking man anymore. Renfield seems more like a mad dog now, ready to hurt anyone that gets in his way.'

CHAPTER THIRTY-TWO

SOME FORTY MINUTES LATER, at just after 5 a.m., a small, serious-faced group of men gathered in the equipment-lined control tower, the nerve centre of the airport.

Gathered round Thane and Moss were Captain Laurent, a short, stout man who was the deputy airport commandant, Superintendent Wilkie, in charge of the Ayrshire police forces now gathered round Prestwick, and two men in service dress, Colonel Levenworth, who was U.S.A.F. commander at the station, and Group Captain Charles, the senior R.A.F. officer available.

Ninety feet above ground level, the control room, like a giant glass-walled hot-house, watched over and dictated the technological miracles which formed the routine life of an airport day.

From the tower one man could, by the flick of a switch, extinguish the scores of lights along the airport's mile-plus main runway and bring shimmering brilliance to a totally different path. Other switches and buttons could close circuits which sounded emergency alarms, summoned details of weather conditions or controlled the constant recordings taken of all ground-to-air instructions.

This early morning, however, the tower had yet another new role to play—manhunt headquarters.

The four tower controllers, however, ignored the strange phenomenon in their midst and continued their task of shepherding aircraft down from the sky onto the runway and giving the "green light" to others setting off on their journeys.

Words in a microphone unleashed an aircraft waiting, straining on the runway, or brought another, patiently circling in the clouds above, the final permission to commence its landing.

Amid the background crackle of radio loudspeakers and the faint, constant hum of electrical apparatus, Colonel Levenworth, the last to arrive after having been hurriedly roused from his bed, was brought up to date by Thane.

'After the shooting, Renfield was last seen running away from the boundary, in towards the centre of the airport area,' explained the detective. 'Since then, in what time we've had, the local police, helped by your men and the R.A.F., have pretty well put a cordon round the north boundaries and on a line with the main runway. Luckily, we managed to cut him off from the other big runway by placing some men at its junction.'

'That means the man's somewhere on the other side of that runway just outside, between there and the northern boundary of the airport,' commented the American.

'That's right. We know he hasn't crossed over the tarmac. The controllers here agreed to keep the runway lights burning... luckily the prevailing wind means that that's path aircraft are using anyway. And we've got, well, sentries I suppose you could call them, posted along its length. There are car and jeep patrols patrolling the whole area.

'The airport police are concentrating on guarding the

actual terminal building and passenger waiting rooms and the disembarking area.

'As far as we know, Renfield's still somewhere out there. And our job is to find him as quickly as possible.'

'That will be no easy task, Chief Inspector,' warned Captain Laurent. Pointing through the glass windows of the tower into the darkness, he went on, 'On the other side of that runway there is an absolute jungle of tarmac, grass, huts of all descriptions and anything up to a hundred parked aircraft. There are scores of places where he could be hiding. And there is always the chance that he has slipped out.'

'There is that chance,' agreed Thane. 'But he is more likely to be lying low somewhere out there.'

Colonel Levenworth, immaculate despite the rushed awakening he had had, pouted his lips thoughtfully.

Gazing at the scores of lights sparkling like sequins in the airport area, he asked, 'What's your idea now, Mr Thane? My boys are itching to go in after this fellow Renfield. The airman he shot is being operated on now by our own doctors over at the base hospital. They say he's in no danger, but he has certainly been damned lucky. When this guy fired at him I guess he didn't care much whether he killed or not. If it hadn't been so darn dark I might well have had a dead man on my hands. So say your piece: We're right with you as far as going for him is concerned.'

Thane glanced at Superintendent Wilkie. The latter, stroking his iron-grey moustache, nodded, and told him, 'Go right ahead, Chief Inspector. It may be my parish we're in, but he's your man. Take him your way. We'll back you.'

Both the Group Captain and the airport official voiced their agreement.

The Glasgow man mentally thanked his stars that he had met with such cooperation, especially from Superintendent

Wilkie. Inter-area jealousy was not unknown in Scotland's police forces, and the position could have been a sticky one out-ranked as he was by the Superintendent and operating outside his own area.

He turned to a large-scale Air Ministry map which Moss, having borrowed it from the tower staff, was now spreading out on a small table.

'Thank you, gentlemen. I have got a rough plan in mind, but I'll be grateful for any suggestions you care to add.

'Our search area forms a blunt "V," the apex being at the main Monkton-Prestwick road, roughly to the west. If our man's still inside—and I believe he is—I think we should treat this as if we were dealing with a speck of dirt in a funnel. We should try to "blow" him out, down towards that road. To do that, however, we need a fair number of men. And, in the opening stages at any rate, we can't spare a single man who is on the cordon at the moment.'

Group Captain Charles, a slim erect figure with a faded row of medal ribbons on his tunic beneath his R.A.F. wings, cleared his throat. 'I can help a little, old man. I've got a flight sergeant rounding up all our stray bodies he can find—if you'll pardon the phrase.'

'We're strained to the limit already, Thane,' said the Superintendent, shaking his head. 'There's one man and a girl left at County Headquarters, and I'm praying that the rest of the countryside behaves itself until this is over.'

'Well, you can have about, say, fifty of my men,' contributed the American, absent-mindedly lighting a cigarette, then, apologetically, offering them round. 'They're guys who weren't on the camp, you know, living out with their families or off base, that sort of thing. I'm keeping only an emergency crew on duty.

'There's something else I'd better get off my chest. I know

you English—O.K., don't jump me, *British*—don't like guns. Some of you think that we Americans become so many juvenile delinquents playing at cowboys and Indians the moment we lay hands on a firearm. But my men are armed. Any others are being armed, carbines mostly, except for the military police. They've got .45 revolvers and night-sticks. I'm sorry, but I'm keeping them that way. For our money it's plain crazy to go after a gun-happy gangster with your bare hands unless you absolutely have to.'

Thane raised an expressive eyebrow towards the R.A.F. officer.

'The guard have their rifles and five rounds each,' shrugged the Group Captain. 'The rest have pick-hafts and that sort of thing. I even saw a couple with golf clubs. But, frankly, I'd feel happier if they all had guns.'

'If it makes you any happier, Mr Thane,' began Colonel Levenworth. The detective cut him short.

'We don't like guns, it's true,' he told the group. 'When bullets fly about it is usually an innocent bystander who gets hurt. But this is an exception. Renfield is armed, and obviously in a state of mind where he'll risk anything. If he's still in our funnel, he may try to blast his way out.

'Meet me halfway. Tell your men, Colonel, and yours, Group Captain Charles, that no one fires a shot under any circumstances unless Renfield shoots first, and that even then they don't shoot to kill. As an individual, I don't honestly care whether we get him dead or alive. But as a policeman, I want him to stand trial.'

'When do we move, then?' asked Wilkie.

'Not much sense in doing anything before dawn,' replied the detective. He glanced at his wristwatch. 'It's coming on for five-thirty. We'll start at seven.'

The next half-hour passed quickly as the leaders of the

various forces prepared their men for the search—named "Operation Strainer" by Inspector Moss in a crack which brought him a sour look from his superior.

A stream of cars and trucks moved on the airport roads carrying men to their positions, many of the vehicles, equipped with radio, taking up posts as section headquarters.

'I could do with some coffee,' declared Colonel Levenworth. 'Being yanked out of bed at this hour is no joke. Say... how about you fellows from Glasgow? I'll bet you could use something substantial. How about a plateful of bacon and eggs? One thing about being at an airport, you know, you can have a banquet at any time of the day or night.'

'I don't mind,' smiled Thane. 'I seem to have been living on sandwiches lately.'

'How about you, Mr Moss?'

'Any chance of something lighter?' asked the inspector wistfully.

'Ulcer man?' queried Levenworth. 'Shake hands with a fellow club member. You're in luck, friend. There's a chef down here who can scramble eggs so that they just float, they're so light. Say, have you tried this latest idea...?'

The two, beaming at the sudden bond between them, drifted away in a closely detailed discussion of diets, drugs and ulcer jokes.

The quick meal had all the quality that had been promised. As they ate, the two detectives watched the everyday work of the airport continue without pause.

Trans-Canada, K.L.M. Royal Dutch, B.O.A.C., Pan-Am— a dozen different lines, a dozen different accents on the air.

The silver planes droned lazily in, then touched down, engines reduced to a still mighty whisper, tyres squealing at their first ninety-mile-an-hour impact with the runway after thousands of miles of cloud-cossetted idleness.

Their passengers were quickly and quietly shepherded the short distance from the apron outside the airport terminal, through Customs and Immigration, and were on their way by car or bus to their destinations before they had time to note the silent cordon of men spaced at intervals all around.

Throughout the airport the bustle continued—cars, lorries, jeeps, patrolling in slow, steady circles. Only the red-painted fire tender, the ambulance, and a few other emergency vehicles stayed with the petrol bowsers at their appointed posts.

The men in the control tower were too far away to hear the sudden crackle of shots from the northeast side of the guarded perimeter, a point nearly a mile away.

A breathless voice, calling from a radio jeep, gave them the news that Renfield had tried to break through the cordon into the farmlands that lay beyond.

'Blue Zebra Two to Tower, Blue Zebra Two to Tower, urgent message. Over,' crackled the loudspeaker on a shelf above the ground controller's desk.

The deputy commandant himself answered the call, and once more the loudspeaker's atmospherics were broken.

'Blue Zebra Two—Corporal Gordon, R.A.F., here. Man has just attempted to break through cordon near farmhouse, three hundred yards from our position. He fired on us when challenged. Shots returned. Man has escaped back into area under cover of dark. Will we follow? Over.'

Captain Laurent glanced at Thane. The latter shook his head. 'Going into the dark like that will serve no purpose. Another half-hour or so, and it will be light. Tell them to stay put, but to keep their eyes skinned.'

The message was passed, and acknowledged in a tone which made it clear that the corporal was quite happy to obey instructions.

'For,' he told the airman by his side, 'after all, I'm due off on leave tomorrow. The old woman wouldn't half give me hell if I played the ruddy hero and landed in hospital with a bullet for my pains, like that Yank did. Reminds me of a time we were out in Egypt, it does. Did I ever tell you about the time we caught the locals trying to flog some stuff from our ration dump?'

'You did, Corp,' sighed his companion. 'But go ahead. At least it'll pass the time.'

Passing the last long minutes before the dawn was also a wearying business at the control tower.

'I wondered when the blighter would put in his next appearance,' mused Group Captain Charles, just returned from a quick tour of guard he had placed across the edge of the runway where it met the Monkton-Prestwick road. 'Now he knows he is trapped. Strange, thinking of him stuck out there like that. He hasn't a hope in hell. Mr Moss—this sort of thing is more up your street than mine. What do you imagine he feels like right now?'

Wrinkling his nose in mental concentration, Moss answered, 'First of all, I don't feel in the least sorry for the swine. Neither would you if it had been one of your airmen he had killed, shot down as if he was a cardboard dummy at a fair-ground sideshow. As for how he feels, well, I've a pretty good idea. Desperate, frightened, angry, uncertain, sorry for himself... the uncertainty is the worst, I'd say.

'I remember going after an escaped convict once. He got away from an outside work party. Jumped a fence and ran... simple as that. The only thing was that he had no friends in the Glasgow area, nobody to take him in and hide him. So he had to stay in the open.

'It took us three days to find him. Finally, he was spotted cutting across a field, and we got him. He had hidden in bushes by day and travelled by night. All he had had to eat was some raw rhubarb from a field, and a pint of milk he stole from a house door. That man struggled when we caught him. But when it was all over, and he was back in the car, being driven towards the prison again, he was laughing and joking. He was really happy. The uncertainty was finished, you see.'

'Hmm....' The Group Captain peered through the control tower windows. 'Blue Zebra Two is the call sign of a jeep I've got stationed just this side of the threshold. Oh, I forgot, you're not an airport type. Do you see that line of green lights? That's the threshold, a sort of front door at the beginning of the runway.

'This fellow Renfield travelled quite a distance to get there from the hangars.'

Moss, standing beside him, gazed at the now greying expanse, on which the airport lights were taking on a more pallid hue, and the first faint outlines of buildings were beginning to appear.

'Not long now,' he murmured. 'I wonder just where he is now.'

Crouched inside the walls of an old, roofless brick shed close by the banks of a stream, the same small stream he had nearly fallen into when he first made his uncertain way to the car park, David Renfield was at that moment about half a mile away.

He was still, as Thane had prophesied, on the north side of the runway, which separated him from the airport buildings and the control tower. The tiny glow from a precious cigarette, carefully cupped between his hands, could not be seen from more than a few feet away.

Greedily, dry-lipped, he sucked smoke into his lungs, slowly, jealously, he let it trickle deliciously into the air again.

He was praying, a numb, repetitive prayer to no god in particular; a prayer that the blind terror and despair that gripped him might find some reason to lift.

Nightmares had firmed to solid reality in the last hour, ever since the moment when the sudden clamour of voices at the hangar had awakened him just in time to the trap into which he had been so blissfully walking.

The Canadian pilot, seemingly strolling unconcernedly at his side, had tried to grapple with him as the voices rang out. But Renfield had managed to drag the automatic from his pocket and in one vicious, fear-strengthened swing had smashed the body of the weapon against Grosvenor's forehead in a bone-jarring blow.

The pilot had collapsed with the suddenness of an abandoned puppet, and as he fell the hunted man had ran in a great blind, heart-pumping, half-circle, spurred on by the sound of whistle-blasts, the roaring of cars and the shouts of his pursuers.

But the noises of pursuit had been growing more distant, and he had become conscious of the lights marking the roadway at the edge of the airport glinting before him, only a few hundred yards distant... and then that challenge had rang out in sharp American tones, and the bulk of the guard had appeared before him.

Renfield had just been able to make out the startling white of teeth and eyes against the dark face, the huge, half-raised truncheon in the airman's hand. The American had hesitated, his other hand fumbling at the holster on his belt—hesitated just as another man had, seemingly long years ago.

The reporter had shot, shot to kill, to blot out not only the guard, but the vision he suddenly raised. And once more it was run, run, run again—back into the cloaking darkness, the harsh blast of the American's pistol spurring him on.

Finally, he could go no further. Head, heart and muscles feeling as if they would burst, the fugitive collapsed on the grass, utterly exhausted, only a score of yards from the tarmac of the runway.

There he had lain, head pillowed on the haversack of money, paralysed by fear and fatigue, on the verge of being physically sick, while one after another three airliners had taxied past towards the airport buildings, their searchlight landing beams forcing him to shut his eyes against their brilliance.

"You fool," he thought bitterly. "You stupid damn fool. It didn't come off. Grosvenor talked to someone, the treacherous ape. Still, you've repaid part of that account."

Renfield could even muster a twisted grin as he recalled the sensation of the automatic smashing against the pilot's head.

Later, his strength gathered once more, he crawled a little way back into the taller grass, and lay in a small hollow, seeing and hearing vehicles moving along the edge of the nearby runway.

"I've got to get out. It can't be so terribly long until dawn now. When that comes, I'm finished. They'll round me up like a stray sheep."

Crouching, crawling on hands and knees at first, Renfield worked his way further and further away from the runway then, keeping the control tower lights at his back, once more headed towards the north boundary.

His clothing was damp and mud-stained from dragging over wet grass and soft earth when he finally, cautiously, rose to his full height and began walking. The fence loomed ahead, the final barrier, only about four feet in height, but stranded with barbed wire.

Renfield slung the haversack further back on his shoulder and began to climb over. His coat caught in the vicious barbs, and the wires creaked as he balanced, trying to free the garment.

The squeak of the wires carried on the night air... and even as he struggled his figure was grasped by the dazzling glare from the twin headlights of a parked vehicle.

There were shouts.

'There he is... Hey! Stop! Don't move!' English voices this time. Feet began pounding on the roadway towards him.

Swaying wildly, precariously on the wires, he snapped off two shots in the direction of the lights, shots which blazed erratically into the night.

Renfield heard the click which denoted an empty magazine, and tumbled off the fence, tearing a long rip in his coat by sheer force to free himself.

He fled, ducking and dodging, chest heaving as he gulped for air, seeking to elude the light. There was the heavy, flat boom of a rifle, and a bullet tore into the turf near his feet. More shots followed. One plucked a red-hot path across his shoulder, cutting the cloth, only searing the skin, but nearly throwing him to the ground.

If the men had followed, they could have caught him within a few hundred yards blind and helpless with fatigue, sweat streaming down his face and running salt-tasting into his mouth. But they didn't, for some reason he couldn't fathom.

On, on, on, he stumbled until he found, of all fantastic things in an airfield, a clump of trees and bushes and the stream, a stream only a few feet across but deep with the rain of the past few days. Taking shelter from its bank, he followed its course, and reached haven behind the walls of the derelict building—an old workmen's shelter, left over from the days of war when the aerodrome was being built.

Since then, more than one vehicle had passed near it, lights blazing, packed with men.

At the sound of the first he had rammed a fresh magazine of bullets into the automatic. But the tyres had whispered over the roadway, the engine had not faltered. And the others which came later had also gone on, their occupants unaware of the frightened man who knelt so close to them in what, but for the gun in one hand, might have been an attitude of supplication.

"If only I knew where I was," he muttered to himself. "If only I knew what lay out there. It'll be dawn soon. They'll come looking then. I've got to get away. I've got to."

He wept. Tears of rage, despair, bitterness at his fate. None of remorse. There was no time for that particular emotion, even if he had felt so inclined. Sardonically, he recalled the words of a magistrate to whom he had often listened in the press benches at court.

"Sorry? Sorry you were caught, you mean," the bewigged, black-gowned figure had castigated the offenders before him.

"If only I'd got away with Grosvenor. Why did that policeman Macrae and that Yank have to get in the way? I didn't want to kill them, they made me do it," he protested to himself. "What am I going to do now? What's going to happen next?"

The cigarette could give only one more draw. Holding the stub in his fingertips, he sucked in the smoke, then squashed the glowing tip on the concrete floor and awaited the daylight.

CHAPTER THIRTY-THREE

AT 7 A.M., the land cold and bleak in the early light, the search began. Slender lines of men—Americans, police, R.A.F. National Service men, armed with everything from rifles to iron bars and batons—began probing the outer areas in the east sector of the airport, using the main runway as their south boundary, the airport perimeter as their northern limit.

Slowly, surely, yard by yard, the ground was pronounced "clear" and the cordon tightened.

In the control tower, Superintendent Wilkie and the airport deputy, Captain Laurent, delegated the job because of their local knowledge, were in charge of the radio link which was the heart of the dragnet.

Thane and Moss joined Colonel Levenworth, who was wearing a gaily decorated flying jacket, and they set off in an Air Force jeep, prowling ahead of the searchers. They were moving slowly along when a strange whirring noise filled the air, causing the two policemen to peer skywards.

'It's a helicopter, Colin!' exclaimed Moss, as a strange

shape rose from the American sector of the airfield and began to beat its lazy way towards them.

'Yes, I forgot to mention it to you, Chief Inspector,' apologised the American. 'I thought one of our choppers might be quite a help, doing a spot of aerial reconnaissance. If nothing else, it will stop the guy from moving about.'

Thane, beginning to feel the effects of little sleep and the strain of the hunt, still managed to grin his admiration at the enterprise. 'We've got to hand it to you, Colonel. One thing I like about you Americans is the way in which you make sure you make the most of your resources.'

They watched the helicopter whirr overhead, low enough for them to make out the jockey-capped pilot and observer in the transparent bubble cockpit. The observer, catching a glimpse of the Colonel in the open jeep, nudged the pilot and pointed. Both lifted their caps in an exaggerated gesture of courtesy to their commanding officer which brought a roar of laughter from the policemen.

Then, the sound of its rotors increasing in volume, the machine slipped away on another tack.

'Tower to Blue Peter One, come in Chief Inspector Thane,' spluttered the loudspeaker of the jeep's radio. Thane unhooked the hand-phone from its holder, flicked down the transmitting switch, then, after a pause to allow the valves to heat, replied.

'Roger, Tower, Blue Peter One here. Over.'

The voice of Captain Laurent came over the air. 'Chief Inspector, a problem. We've got about a dozen press men, reporters and photographers in the airport lounge at the moment. Rumours of what's going on seem to be spreading all over the district. What do you want us to do? Some of the fellows seem to know it's Renfield we're after. Over.'

Thane's face darkened. 'Herd them all into a hotel room

and keep them there. Put a couple of police on the door... and shove any other newsmen that come along in beside them,' he rapped. 'Tell them that I guarantee they'll get the full story after the search, but that any man found on the runway is liable to be put in a cell—and I'll personally throw away the key.'

He had known that the manhunt, on such a gigantic scale, could not be kept secret for long. The way in which hundreds of men had cheerfully volunteered to search for a man whom they knew might shoot on sight was a story he was determined must be told.

But Colin Thane wasn't going to have a mess of reporters and photographers turning the hunt into a three-ring newspaper circus—especially when the man he sought was a friend of many of their number.

While the protesting newspapermen were being shepherded into a large room at the hotel and being consoled, at the airport authorities' expense, with tea, beer and sandwiches, the ragged eastern ends of the cordoned area had already been completely searched by the long line of uniformed men, probing in huts and trenches, even clambering into parked aircraft in case Renfield had climbed aboard and was trying to hide until they passed.

The gaps between them narrowed. The funnel down which the man they sought was to be "blown" was now a reality.

A thin drizzle began to add to the gloom of the hour. Heavier clouds were building up on the skyline. Thane glanced apprehensively at the far end of the runway, down which the jeep was slowly moving, driving on the right-hand side, the international rule of the road, applied inside airports everywhere.

'Relax, Chief Inspector,' said the American, noticing his

movement. 'If it's aircraft you're thinking of, there's nothing due in or out for the next hour or so. This is always the quietest time in the air. We should be all tidied up, I guess, before things get busy.'

'It was worrying me,' admitted Thane. 'The idea of being chased down this path by eighty tons of Stratocruiser doesn't appeal to me. This damned weather doesn't make me any happier either.'

'Nor me,' chimed in Moss. 'What wouldn't I give for a nice warm cuppa. How long is this runway anyway, Colonel? Looks a tremendous stretch from here.'

'Roughly a mile, Mr Moss. This is the main runway we're on now. It is all of three hundred feet wide, and one of the best landing strips in the U.K., thanks to the fantastic fog-free weather you Scots have in this corner. There's... Say, what's that crazy chopper driver doing?' he suddenly barked.

The helicopter, which had been weaving some distance ahead of the searchers, over the grassland area, had suddenly brought in full power, and with a beat of rotors was heading fast and low towards the runway.

'Let's follow her,' exclaimed Thane. 'The pilot must have seen something.'

As the American slammed the jeep into gear and gunned the motor the radio called, 'Tower to Blue Peter One, come in, urgent.'

'Go ahead, Tower. Over,' shouted Thane over the handset as the jeep bucked off the tarmac in pursuit of the helicopter which was now hovering over a spot about three hundred yards distant and about two hundred yards north of the runway.

'Thane, Superintendent Wilkie here,' came the response. 'The helicopter pilot has radioed he is positive they saw something moving among the bushes down beside the Pow Burn—that's the little stream north of the main runway. Over.'

'Going there now,' confirmed Thane, then hung on to his seat as the jeep pranced over another patch of rough ground.

Next moment the little vehicle braked to a standstill on the edge of the bushy copse through which the burn flowed. The helicopter had landed on the opposite bank, as near as safety would permit.

Behind, the sound of other vehicles dashing to the scene could be heard. As the three men scrambled from the jeep the observer came running from the grounded chopper and, standing on the opposite bank, shouted over the hollow.

'We saw the guy. I'm sure we did. Just for a minute. He came from somewhere that way.' He waved downstream. 'I just got a glimpse of him, and then the goddam line of the ground got in the festering way.'

'Show me,' called Thane, and, one on either bank, he and the overalled airman dashed across the uneven ground.

'Just about here, Mac,' called the observer, coming to a halt about fifty yards downstream. 'Say, maybe he was holed up in that brick shack over here. You can cross over at the little bridge up there.'

The jeep, which had been hurriedly turned by the Colonel, pulled in beside Thane.

'Over the bridge, Colonel,' instructed the detective, jumping aboard, and with a jerk the drab little workhorse sped over the short distance, then bumped back up the other bank.

Pulling his gun from his pocket, Thane leapt off as the jeep stopped, and, with a surprising agility for his build, scrambled down the bank towards the brick structure and disappeared into it.

Thane burst into the brick shell quite prepared to find Renfield crouching behind the walls, hoping only that he would take him by surprise before he could use his gun.

A damp gabardine raincoat lay in one corner, showing he

had been there all right—but the reporter had gone. The detective emerged again, just as the helicopter's crewman and the Colonel slithered down the bank.

'Been—and gone,' he told the two Americans. 'Where's Inspector Moss?'

'I left him where we first stopped,' explained Colonel Levenworth. 'Hey, look, he's at that bridge, trying to attract our attention.'

Moss's figure was behaving in an excited manner, his arms waving above his head, as he beckoned them back.

'Jump in and hang on,' cried Levenworth, thoroughly enjoying himself. Thane and the observer were still boarding the jeep when he crunched into reverse gear. One hand on the wheel, gazing backwards over his shoulder, the Colonel sent it whining back the short distance across the grass at a fast, slightly weaving pace which brought harsh, protesting noises from the transmission.

'What's up, Phil?' asked Thane, as the machine came to a halt beside the inspector.

'Look down there,' Moss told him, eyes fixed along the course of the stream. 'This isn't a bridge. It's the entrance to a culvert.'

Thane followed his gaze and whistled. The Pow Burn, several feet broad at this point and swollen by the recent rain, flowed straight in the direction of the main runway, went under the old stone bridge some distance before the runway's edge, and, instead of reappearing, slid into a broad, high tunnel.

'He might be in there,' agreed Thane. 'I wonder where the hell it goes to?'

'Clean under the runway and out some distance beyond,' said a quiet American voice behind them. 'Have a coffin nail.'

The observer from the helicopter was holding out a battered packet of Lucky Strike.

Ignoring the offered cigarette, Thane pounced on his words. 'You're sure? Could a man get through?'

'I'm sure. I did a spell of duty with the gasoline bowsers. They lie just short of the exit on a tarmac park. The number of kids we caught sneaking up that tunnel was nobody's business. Mind you, that was in the summer, when there was only a few inches of water in the stream.'

He stopped for a moment as two carloads of men who had rushed towards the scene drew to a halt a few yards away. Then another thought struck him.

'Say, that cordon you've got round here... the culvert leads out well beyond it, way on the other side of the runway. If the guy you're after is in there, he'll get clean away.

'In fact, it pops up right on the airport edge, beside a housing scheme. Glenburn they call it. And if he's a smart cookie he'll keep right on going till he's outside the area altogether.'

The two detectives gazed at each other, dismayed. Moss pounded hand and fist together.

Thane moved first. Taking two steps towards the jeep, he lifted the radio handset from its place and pressed the microphone button.

'Blue Peter One to Tower. Renfield believed escaping through Pow Burn culvert under runway. It will take him beyond cordon. Rush some men to the other end. Over.'

The Tower answered immediately. 'We're getting them there now. Damn sorry, Thane. We forgot all about that tunnel. Out now.'

'Colonel, do you know the other end of the culvert?' asked Thane. The officer shook his head.

'I'll take him, Colonel,' volunteered the other American.

The driving seat was hurriedly vacated, and the airman got behind the wheel.

'Stay here, Phil, with the men that have just come up,' ordered Thane. 'Watch this end with the Colonel.'

He turned to the new driver. 'Let's go.'

They stormed along a perimeter track leading to the runway, on across it, past a puzzled airman on watch there, roared over the three-hundred-foot width, then took another narrow track.

The jeep's horn blared, and a group of men in R.A.F. blue, carrying rifles and pick-hafts and running in the same direction, scattered to let the vehicle whizz past.

At the edge of the culvert exit, another brick and concrete structure, the jeep braked to a jarring halt. Not far away, smoke was curling from a farm cottage chimney. Cattle stood in a cluster on the other side of a fence only a few yards distant, a fence which marked the edge of the airport. A small green G.P.O. van stood empty a little way up the road which ran by the cottage. In the far background lay the rows of council houses.

Here the Pow waters once more returned to daylight, coming out of the culvert in a quick-moving mud-coloured flow which eddied as the natural bed of the stream once more took charge of its direction and sent it winding away into the distance.

All seemed quiet. Thane scrambled down the sloping grass bank and peered into the dark tunnel, which appeared divided into three sections by concrete pillars. He could see nothing.

Clawing his way once more up the bank, he met the interested gaze of the American. 'If he's in there, he'll be kinda wet by now,' drawled the Yank. 'We've come 'bout a quarter-mile, I'd guess. Pretty rough going through that tunnel.'

'If you were as desperate as he is,' said Thane, 'you'd be willing to try it.'

The R.A.F. men, flush-faced excited youngsters, arrived on the scene, and the corporal in charge spread them out on both banks, watching, waiting. Once more Thane went down the bank. This time, fingers gripping a projecting ledge, he put his head inside the left-hand tunnel.

'Come out, Renfield, you're trapped,' he yelled. 'Give up, you fool.'

The silence within was broken only by the faint gurgling of the water.

'There's three separate wee tunnels all the way through, sir,' piped one aircraftsman. 'If he's in one of the others, he won't hear you. I'll try.'

Suiting his words, the youngster scrambled down the opposite bank, and, balancing precariously over the water, yelled into the dark right-hand mouth, 'Hey, come on out o' there or we'll come in an'...'

Before he finished the roar of a shot sounded from within the tunnel, then the whine of a ricochet came from the entrance.

The aircraftsman gave a screech of surprise, overbalanced, and hit the water with a splash. He went under, coming up next moment roaring but unhurt. Wringing wet, he practically flew out of the water and up the bank, a comical sight but for the nearness of his escape.

'Jeeze-oh!' he gulped.

As his companions crowded round the soaking airman Thane saw a middle-aged man, wearing chest-high black rubber waders running clumsily along the road from the farm cottage, obviously moving as quickly as the cumbersome garment would allow.

'What's up?' shouted the man as he drew near. 'Is something wrong with the boy?'

'What boy?' asked Thane.

'Laurie—I left him in the tunnel. What's going on, mister, what's all the commotion?'

'Better tell me what you're talking about first. Did you leave someone here?' asked the detective.

'Aye, I did. Just five minutes ago. I'd better away up to him.' The man made to scramble down the bank, but Thane gripped his arm, holding him back.

'You can't go in there. A man with a gun's loose in that tunnel. Take it easy. Who's this lad you left? What are you doing here?'

Gulping, pale-faced, the man in the high waders explained, 'My name's McNeil—Tom McNeil. I'm a Post Office engineer. We're down to check over some telecommunications lines that run through the aerodrome, you know, phones and printers and things. There's a junction box on the culvert roof at one point. The lad and I—his name's Laurie Blane—came down about half an hour ago to start the job. The junction box in the tunnel...'

'Which tunnel?' demanded Thane.

'The one on the right there,' replied McNeil. 'I was going to say that the box is away up on the roof, where the water never reaches it, though there's a waterproof casing cover, just in case.'

'The right-hand tunnel is the one the man we're looking for is in, I'm afraid,' the detective told him. 'What was the boy doing?'

'I left Laurie unfastening the waterproof cover while I went up to that cottage to get some hot water for tea. We left without any breakfast this morning. He was all right. There's a little iron ranged ladder up to the box, and there's a sort of ledge at the top to lay tools. I was just coming to tell him to knock off for a bit, as the woman in the cottage was making the tea, when I saw you fellows.'

'Is that your van there?' asked Thane.

'Yes,' replied McNeil. 'It's easier leaving it there and just hopping over the fence to the culvert. Less trouble usually, than having to go through all sorts of red tape before we can drive through the airport. But here, how about Laurie? Can't we go in and see about getting him out? I've got a spare pair of waders in the van.'

'Do you see that airman—the youngster with the wet clothing?' asked Thane. 'He was going to have a look in the tunnel—and he nearly got his head shot off for his trouble.'

'We'll need to do something,' protested McNeil. 'Laurie's only a kid of sixteen. How bad a bloke is the fellow that's in there?'

'Nearly as bad as they come,' replied Thane. 'But stay here, and keep your fingers crossed. I'm going to have a try at getting them both out.'

He slithered down the grass bank again, cautiously approached the right-hand tunnel entrance, and shouted in, 'Renfield, it's Thane. Don't shoot.... I want to talk to you. It's about the boy.'

'Go ahead,' came a muffled shout from within. 'I can hear you... but don't try coming in. I've got him here. And he gets the next bullet.'

'Send him out, David,' pleaded Thane. 'He's only a kid. He's done nothing. You're in big enough trouble without adding more to it. Send the lad out. Then come out and surrender yourself. We've got both ends of the culvert watched. There's nothing more you can do.'

'Come in and get me,' Renfield shouted an invitation. 'The

first move you make, the boy gets his. Yell out, boy, tell them what's happened.'

A fainter, boyish voice stammered, 'I'm all right, Tom. But he's got a gun.'

'Hear that, Thane? He's all right—so far. Tell you what I'll do. Let me come out of the culvert, call off your watch, and I'll turn him loose as soon as I get clear of the neighbourhood. He won't be harmed—if you do what I tell you.'

'We can't do that, David, you know that,' shouted Thane.

'Can't you? Then if anything happens to him it's your fault as much as mine. Think it over.' Renfield's voice stopped, there was silence from the tunnel once more. Thane clambered up the bank, and faced the anxious engineer.

'You heard?'

'Aye,' nodded McNeil. 'What are you going to do? You'll need to let him get away, won't you?'

Slowly, reluctantly, Thane shook his head. 'We can't.'

'What about Laurie—you can't just leave him,' protested the horrified engineer.

'I don't know. We'll get him out somehow. But we can't bargain with the man holding him.'

As the engineer, anxious, bewildered, stared at the Chief Inspector a police car drove along the narrow road and stopped just short of the culvert exit. Out of it stepped Moss, Superintendent Wilkie and a civilian. Thane met them a few yards from where the airmen and the engineer waited.

'He's in there all right,' he told the new arrivals. 'And there's the very devil of a complication. He's got a young G.P.O. apprentice in there, and is holding him at gun-point. The boy was starting some cable repairs. Renfield's trying to use his safety as a lever to force us to let him get away.'

Superintendent Wilkie cursed and blushed at the same time. 'I blame myself for this mess,' he admitted. 'And now this poor youngster... heavens, when I was a boy I used to paddle in the Pow. But I forgot all about this damn tunnel. They only began building it during the war.'

'That's the reason for Mr Petrie being here,' he added, gesturing towards the plump, elderly man in the lounge suit at his side. 'Mr Petrie's a Ministry of Civil Aviation type, and knows the layout of most of the construction work on the aerodrome. He can tell you all about the tunnel.'

The drizzle of rain had begun once more. Calling McNeil, the Post Office engineer, over to join them, the little party went back to the car and crowded inside it for shelter. Petrie, borrowing Moss's notebook, began to make a rough pencil sketch, explaining as he did so.

'This culvert is really three big drainpipes,' he told them. 'It runs, as you know, from just below Aitkenbrae bridge... here... under the runway, continues under these hard standings and grasslands, and comes up... here... at Shaw Cottage.'

'How long altogether, Mr Petrie?' asked Thane.

'Close on 1,200 feet, I'd say, Chief Inspector. Call it a bit under a quarter of a mile. It was mainly built during the war, of course, and not one in a hundred Prestwick people know of it. Though what they think happens to the burn I can't imagine.

'As far as the structure is concerned, well, take this as a side view.' His pencil raced over the paper once more. 'The entrance roof is five feet below runway level, and the actual culvert is about five feet eight inches in height and nearly thirty feet across. There are two supporting concrete walls running along its length. You've really got an oblong-shaped structure, divided into three long tunnels, the middle one about seven feet wide, the other two about six feet.'

'No connecting hatches?'

'None,' replied Petrie. 'There are one or two small drainpipes running into the tunnel here and there, but they're only a few inches in diameter. Oh, as far as the level is concerned, there's a very slight fall to assist the flow, only a few inches in the whole length, and the tunnel height does drop just a little the last hundred feet or so before the exit. But that's all. So this man you're after would have no trouble in getting through, apart from the cold and wet.' He shivered at the thought.

'Mr McNeil,' demanded Thane. 'Whereabouts is this junction box of yours?'

'About here,' said the engineer, pointing to the rough plan. 'About four hundred feet from the exit point. This gunman must have marched young Laurie along towards the entrance.'

'How about lights? Are there any lights fitted at any part of the tunnel?'

'None. I left an electric hand-lamp with young Laurie. But there's nothing else in there, no lights at all.'

'In that case,' said Thane, 'there's only one thing for it. Driver, take the car to the upstream entrance to the tunnel. I'm going in after Renfield—I'll try and sneak up on him from the rear.'

CHAPTER THIRTY-FOUR

THANE'S WORDS brought a storm of protests from his companions. Moss, ignoring the Superintendent's presence, objected, 'You're daft, Colin. The man can't stay there forever. He's got to come out sooner or later. Why not wait for him?'

'If he was alone, I'd agree. There would be a dozen methods we could use—pump smoke or tear gas in, that sort of thing— to force him out into the open without risk to anyone.

'But there's this boy to think of. Renfield is gambling with young Blane's life. If he finds his gamble isn't coming off... well, he said himself, the lad gets the next bullet. We can't let him walk out of there with the boy as hostage, and if we keep him penned in we may be sacrificing the youngster's life. Young Blane's only chance of safety is for someone to slip through the tunnel and nail Renfield.'

'Then I'll come too,' announced Moss, unhappily loyal.

'Aren't you the man who boasts he can't swim a stroke?' smiled Thane. 'Thanks, Phil, but this is my own particular pigeon. Mr McNeil, how high would you say the water was in the tunnel?'

The Post Office engineer glanced at the chest-high waders he was still wearing and replied, 'About— Say a little over three feet, sir. The water's higher than usual just now because of all the rain there's been of late. The current's not terribly strong, though. The main force of the burn goes through the other two channels of the culvert.'

'Three feet,' echoed Thane. 'That's what I mean, Phil. From what Mr McNeil says, I should be able to more or less walk all the way. But it may come to swimming. And that would make you worse than useless.'

'Take some of my men then,' urged the Superintendent. 'There are several first-class swimmers among them.'

'Thanks for the offer. But the more there are, the less chance of getting near Renfield and catching him unawares and the greater risk of his harming young Blane. We want no casualties that can possibly be avoided.'

Reluctantly they agreed.

'That's settled. Now, Superintendent, I want you, if you will, to create a diversion. Stay here and haggle with Renfield. Pretend we're on the brink of accepting his terms. Stall for time, as long as you can. While his attention is fixed on your end of the tunnel, I'll be coming down from his rear.'

Superintendent Wilkie nodded in understanding, and left the car, walking briskly over towards the culvert exit. Seconds later the Jaguar's engine came to life, and the car purred towards Aitkenbrae bridge and the upstream entrance.

In the dank cold of the tunnel, the light from a battery-powered hand-lamp pushing the darkness back only a few feet, David Renfield stood on one of the rungs of the little iron ladder which led to the cable junction box in the roof, gun pointed squarely towards the pale-faced youngster perched beside him. The boy seemed unable to take his eyes away from the automatic, hypnotised by the menace only inches away.

Despite the ladder, which lifted him almost completely out of the water, the numbing chill of the flow swirling round his ankles caused Renfield's whole body to shiver as he waited, uncertain as to his next move.

'What's your name?' he asked his hostage.

'Laurie, mister. Laurie Blane. What are you going to do with me, mister?' asked the boy, lips trembling.

'That all depends on the police out there, Laurie,' Renfield told him. 'If they let me go, then I'll take you with me and turn you loose after I'm clear. If they don't, you heard what I said.'

'But I've done nothing, mister,' pleaded the young apprentice. 'Let me go and I won't tell them anything.'

'You don't understand, boy,' said Renfield, voice growing weary. 'The police know I've killed a man already. That's why they aren't coming in after me. That's why, right now, they are probably deciding to let me out. If they come in, I kill you. If they don't let me out, I kill you. Simple, isn't it?

'They still hang some murderers, you know. That's what I am, a murderer, though I didn't want to kill that man either. Even if they don't hang you, they send you to prison for what they call "life"—fifteen years. If you behave, you may even get out after ten years. For what I did, though, it's still the rope—and as far as I'm concerned, I'd rather choose a quick end than all that time behind bars.

'No wonder they call it "life." It leaves just an empty husk of a man. Do you know what happens to people after a long spell inside? Either they end up in a padded cell, singing psalms all day, or they come out shattered shadows of what they were. Only the stupid can emerge intact. Only the people who can't think, who can't realise what has happened to them.

And I'm not stupid. Sure, the police have me trapped here. But that was only luck.'

The boy, quivering, staring blankly at him as Renfield, chill cold seeping through his body, went on, 'There's a man called Thane out there—Chief Detective Inspector Thane of the C.I.D. I made him look a fool, even found witnesses for him and pretended to be trying to help. I don't know how he finally caught on to the fact that I was the man he wanted. But I nearly got away with it.

'Do you see this haversack? I've got £6,500 in it. A lot of money, eh? I had to kill a man to get it, I've told you. And I'll kill another man if necessary to keep it and my freedom. You can understand that, can't you?'

For Renfield, the tunnel had been a last, unconvincing hope. For over an hour he had lain within almost a stone's throw of the culvert entrance, not knowing it existed out there in the darkness.

Only when dawn had broken had he first seen the shape of the "bridge," which was its entrance, and, under the arch, the trio of holes into which the water disappeared. He had had no idea where it led to, nor whether it was possible to get through at all. For all he was aware, it might have narrowed down into thin pipes after only a few yards.

But, peering out of the doorway of the brick shed, he had seen the long line of men slowly advancing, and realised that discovery was only a matter of time. He had shed his coat then, in case it hampered him in the water. He had taken several rolls of five-pound notes and thrust them into his trouser and jacket pockets, in case he had to abandon the haversack and its bulky contents.

Quitting his cover, Renfield slid into the bitter, muddy water and waded into the furthest away tunnel mouth, where the flow appeared to be the least turbulent. The reporter had held his automatic high in one hand to keep it clear of the stream as, other hand feeling along the culvert wall, he had waded on, head almost touching the roof, water swirling around his waist.

After forty yards or so the glow of light from the entrance completely faded, and he was in a darkness which grew steadily blacker, until the walls, even the water lapping around him, were swallowed up in the inky blackness. He kept on his blind path... struck by the sudden fear that the tunnel might go on and on until it came out somewhere under the sea. But the water level had risen no further. Air seemed to be blowing along the damp interior of the culvert.

Then he had seen the gleam in the distance, and had struggled on towards it, at first imagining it marked the tunnel exit.

As he approached nearer, however, Renfield saw that the light came from a small electric lamp, held by a youth in rubber waders. The boy, standing on the rungs of an iron ladder set in the concrete wall, was working slowly and painstakingly with a spanner, loosening the metal studs on a panel set high to one side of the culvert roof.

It had been easy to come up behind the boy and order him down. The youngster had nearly fallen off the iron rungs at the shock of the sudden command barked at him and the sight of the desperate, water-soaked figure wading beneath, gun in hand.

Young Blane walking in front, Renfield had continued towards the tunnel entrance, carrying the lamp in one hand, the automatic jammed firmly against the boy's back.

And he found the exit guarded. The shot he fired over the

boy's shoulder was more in general despair rather than at the faint blob of a target far ahead.

The sound of Thane's voice, echoing up the tunnel, had provided him with another shock. But quickly, quickly as any cornered animal seeing a chance, he had decided to use the boy as a lever. Would he shoot him? 'Only one thing matters. I come first,' he mumbled to himself.

So, after presenting his ultimatum to Thane, he had forced the reluctant apprentice along the tunnel again, back to the ladder.

Together they had climbed as far out of the water's reach as they could, until their heads touched the top of the little underground dome in which the cable box lay.

He still had the money. He grinned humourlessly. It lay, sodden and cold, in the haversack slung over his jacket, in odd bundles in his suit pockets.

The haversack was uncomfortable. It was now doubly heavy. But he was damned if he would throw it away. It stood for all the things that had nearly happened... things like Jean marrying him. His mind began drifting aimlessly over what might have been.

Partly muffled by the gurgling water, a voice finally shouted from the tunnel exit. 'Renfield, Renfield, it's the police again. We want to talk to you.'

'Down,' gestured the fugitive. 'We'll see what they want. Move... I haven't all day.'

He waved the gun. The boy, nervously obeying, dropped down into the water and, Renfield once more carrying the lamp, they moved a short distance towards the tunnel exit, stopping more than two hundred feet away.

'Renfield. We want to speak to you,' came the voice again.

'Who's that...is it Thane?' he shouted back.

'Renfield, I'm Superintendent Wilkie, in charge of this area. Is the boy still all right?'

'A Superintendent now, Laurie, we're going up in the world,' said the reporter softly. Then, shouting again, 'He's alright. Do you agree to call off your men and let me leave the tunnel? Remember, the boy's safety depends on it.'

'What guarantee have we that you won't shoot him once you are loose?' countered the policeman, playing for time.

'None. Only my word, which probably isn't particularly valued,' retorted the reporter. 'But he won't be hurt if you let me get clear. And you know the alternative. What about it? It's cold in here. I'm not going to wait forever.'

'Where would you let him go?'

'How the hell do I know?' bellowed Renfield. 'Once I get well away from the airport. Once I know there are no police around to grab me.'

CHAPTER THIRTY-FIVE

COLIN THANE, stripped down to shirt and trousers, stepped off the bank into the water and gasped as the chill struck him. He still wore his shoes, because of the numerous sharp stones which, he had been warned, studded the floor of the culvert.

Thane was moving quickly, despite the fact that the roof of the tunnel was so low that he had to crouch a little to prevent his head banging against it.

He kept one hand on the slime-darkened concrete wall, just as, unknown to him, Renfield had done. An unlit electric torch was in his left hand. He dare not use it—but it might be needed before this grim underground adventure was played to a finish.

Rubbing his chin along the top of his left shoulder, he felt the cold butt of his revolver, strapped there by an arrangement of string and handkerchiefs to keep it high and dry.

Splashing on, he cursed as his feet slipped on a boulder, sending him nearly sprawling into the water. But Thane regained his balance and, once more, the current of the stream pressing him forward, he continued his slow journey.

"Must be under the main runway now," he thought to himself. "Damn silly business, this, practically swimming under an aerodrome. Wonder what the pilots would think?"

Nearly at the halfway mark now, he reckoned. Somewhere, not far ahead, the man he sought must be waiting, perhaps already having heard him coming, letting him draw nearer to make a better target.

Must be getting close... He stumbled on, hugging the wall, feet slipping on the stone-covered bottom.

'Wonder how Renfield's making out in this—he must be freezing,' he growled, then suddenly realised he had been talking aloud.

The strain was telling, without a doubt, the strain of waiting for a shot that hadn't come, for a splash or rustle that meant Renfield was close ahead.

"Snap out of it. You're getting as bad as old Moss," he told himself.

Slop, slop, slop, the water went around him. He had practically lost all feeling in his legs. They just kept moving in a mechanical fashion.

Thane saw the light ahead before he heard the voices, a glow in the otherwise impenetrable darkness. Then he heard the muffled shouts and realised that Superintendent Wilkie was still playing his part.

Carefully now... closer... closer.

'What's your answer, Superintendent?' he heard Renfield shout. He could make out the two figures ahead of him now, silhouettes against the lamp shining towards the tunnel exit.

"If I could knock that light out," mused Thane. "Or if I could grab Renfield... but could I get close enough without being heard?"

'What's your answer?' yelled Renfield again, now only some thirty feet away.

Thane stepped slowly forward, every move seeming to raise a thunder of splashes.

"My God, surely he can hear me," he thought. Nearer... nearer... he pulled the revolver from its makeshift holster.

'We need time to think,' hailed Wilkie from the tunnel exit.

Viciously the fugitive hurled his retort, 'Five minutes... then the boy gets a bullet.' Harshly he ordered the slightly built figure at his side, 'Get back to the ladder.'

Fifteen feet. There was no time now for fancy plans. As Renfield turned, the torch still blazing, but the gun no longer pointed towards the boy, Thane shouted, shouted louder than he would have thought possible, 'Drop it, Renfield. It's Thane!'

At the shout, Renfield, jumping to one side, extinguished the light and triggered the automatic in one swift, startled series of moves. The beam, flickering down the walls ahead, had glanced on Thane's figure at almost the same second as the bewildering challenge had rang out.

Flame lanced from the gun, and the boom of the explosion, multiplied over and over again in the tunnel, rang and sang in his ears, while Thane, in the sudden darkness, sensed the passage of the bullets only inches to his left.

'Run, boy!' he called. A swift, frenzied splashing filled the silence as the apprentice, ignored by Renfield in the desperate emergency, stumbled blindly down the tunnel.

'I've let him go, Thane,' came a tired voice from the dark ahead. 'Now it's just you and me.'

Standing motionless, his very breathing seeming loud and magnified, Thane slid the safety catch on his revolver to the "off" position. The click was as if a door had been slammed. Still he remained where he was. Then he shouted, 'Give it up, David. Stop this senseless shooting.'

Even as his voice echoed, the light ahead flicked on once

more, another shot flared. He felt the bullet sting a raking path along his ribs, heard it spit like an angry wasp against the tunnel wall.

Before the thunder of the first shot died, Thane fired twice, two quick shots towards the light. The lamp flickered skywards, then fell into the water, extinguishing almost immediately as it sank beneath the surface.

The detective hurriedly moved his position, crossing from right to left, the water splashing over his shoulders, spraying up into his mouth and eyes, so violent was his rush.

There was no answering shot. There was no cry of pain, no shout of anger. Nothing but the lapping of the water. He peered vainly ahead, not daring to use his torch, keyed to an almost nerve-breaking pitch of expectancy, ears straining.

It seemed fifteen minutes—though probably it was less than three—before he suddenly picked up a slightly louder splash above the murmur of the stream.

It might be a rat, even, perhaps, a fish that was managing to survive in the polluted water.

The second splash was nearer, much nearer. Was he imagining it, or could he really hear a rasping breathing?

He pressed the torch button, and in almost the same second dived under the water as the light showed a white, desperate face, a poised gun, less than ten feet away. Even as the water went over his head he felt rather than heard the two blasts from Renfield's automatic.

The torch lay at the bottom of the culvert. His gun was still in his hand... soaked and useless.

David Renfield was in almost as desperate a position.

He had had only five bullets in his automatic when

Thane's voice had first rung out. There was another clip of ammunition all right... in his hip trouser pocket, saturated by water.

He had let the boy go. It would have been easy to kill him as he splashed his noisy, clumsy escape. But Thane was there... Thane, who symbolised the collapse of all his dreams. Thane, who had fooled him. It was Thane he must kill.

But as for the second time his lamp caught the detective's figure in the darkness, and the automatic kicked in his hand, his foot slipped on a stone.

The two answering shots from Thane's gun, frightful in their nearness, had come just as he was fighting to retain his balance—and the lamp had dropped from his hand.

Now his opponent had the only light. Now Renfield was the mouse waiting for the cat.

But what if the mouse nipped the cat first? He decided to take the war to Thane, torch or no torch.

Pushing against the current at every step, nearly collapsing with cold, keeping going through some strange, twisted purpose, he moved cautiously on. Then the beam of light hit him, he fired twice towards it—and Thane had slipped under the water, the torchlight had gone, and darkness had returned. The policeman might be wounded or even dead. Or he might be waiting, listening, just as he was.

One bullet left. His eyes darted round and saw nothing. His ears heard no more splashes.

Thane, useless gun held clubbed in one hand, only his head above water as he crouched, felt sure the mere sound of his pounding heart must be loud enough to be heard.

Splash! Renfield had moved. He must be just ahead. He could hear his rasping breathing.

Another sound—just ahead now, and slightly to the right. "Hardly more than two yards away," he told himself.

Gathering every fraction of strength left in his chilled body, Thane lunged forward in a final gamble.

His feet pushed him off the concrete floor like a springboard. His body smashed into the water and under, his legs thrashing. Like a human torpedo, the policeman smashed into Renfield's thighs. The gun in the reporter's hand exploded harmlessly roof ward as he overbalanced and fell.

The surface of the water churned as Thane seized his quarry round the waist while Renfield kicked and struggled to free himself.

Both men were below the surface, rolling over and over in the fury of their battle.

With a mighty heave, Renfield forced his way to the surface. Even as his head broke water and he gulped in air he brought his gun blindly down in a short clubbing blow towards his opponent's body.

The metal smashed into Thane's shoulder. But the sodden clothing, the water, Renfield's sapped strength, took all the sting from the impact.

It was Thane's turn to snatch precious air before once more the two men rolled under the surface.

Shifting his grip, Thane strove to wrap his legs round Renfield in a scissors hold, one hand buried in the folds of the reporter's jacket, the other feeling blindly for his throat.

There was sudden searing agony as Renfield's knee sank into his stomach. But before the jab could be repeated, even as he fought against the sickening pain wave, his grasping fingers found the reporter's mouth, and pulled, pulled and twisted at the flesh till it stretched like rubber, while Renfield's two hands abandoned all but the endeavour to relieve the racking torture.

Thane let go, sought for a throat-grip again, achieved his scissors hold, even as a redness came before his eyes, a drumming sounded in his ears.

They rolled again, Thane underneath, then on top, the water above churning to an unseen foam. Renfield's fingers clawed wildly at the detective's face, the nails tearing long scores in the flesh as they searched for the yolk of the eyes.

Thane tried to slam a punch into the man with his failing strength, but the water made it a mockery of a blow. He tried again, this time the flat of his left hand, hard and edged, smashed against Renfield's unguarded throat.

Circles of light were exploding in his head. The air was bubbling from his lungs, he swallowed water. Suddenly the struggles of his opponent became more desperate, less purposeful, frantic. And then he was hitting at a limp figure.

Barely conscious, Thane shook himself free, forced himself to his feet, water pouring from his clothes. He gulped air, retched, gulped again, ears singing, head reeling. Blindly he staggered about until his hands felt the concrete of the wall. He leaned against it, sobbing for breath.

Then there were strong arms round him, a soft Ayrshire voice told him, 'Easy, sir, easy. It's all over.'

They half-carried him out into the daylight, the policeman and the airman. They laid him down on the grassy bank. Moss, who had led the small party in a floundering dash up the tunnel from the exit, stood anxiously over him.

The inspector had dashed to the tunnel exit as soon as the first shot was fired, and had had to be forcibly restrained from charging to his chief's aid when the young apprentice had staggered out to safety. When the shots ended, and the faint sounds of struggle had begun to come through the tunnel, there had been no holding him back.

A look of relief shone from his face as Thane, face filmed in blood from the deep scores scratched on its surface, coaxed a faint, painful grin to life and hoarsely whispered, 'Hello, Phil, how about a cuppa?'

Later, they searched the tunnel once more. They found Renfield's body lying on the bottom. There was nothing that could be done for him, except bring him into the open and cover his face with a greatcoat.

The haversack of money, sodden and torn, still lay round the body. Soaked bundles of notes, spilled from his pockets, floated down the stream. The weight of saturated paper had hindered his struggles, slowed his resistance—and helped to drown him.

The story that was told to the released press men an hour later by a dried and rested Thane, dressed in borrowed American slacks, shirt, and pullover, caused a sensation that made headlines throughout the country.

In the *Evening View* office, the stunning news that David Renfield had been a killer, and the report of his underground death, took some time to sink in.

When it did, there was something close to tears in McRowder's eyes. Renfield had been one of his best men— though he would never have dreamed of admitting it. He disguised his feelings behind a roaring rage.

'We haven't got a picture of the man!' he stormed. 'One of our own staff... and not a solitary picture for the paper!'

THANE & MOSS RETURN IN...

Death Department

PRAISE FOR BILL KNOX

'Bill Knox writes with the factual accuracy of a good reporter. He does his homework thoroughly.'

Evening Times, Glasgow

'His plotting is impeccable... and he can build his books to a relentless climax.'

New York Times Book Review

'The expertise is interesting, the invention good and the writing literate and lively.'

Sunday Times

'Always a thoroughly reliable, good read.'

The Times

'Sound technical details... thrills without frills.'

Sunday Telegraph

'The only practitioner who writes with complete authority and accuracy about the police procedures of Scotland.'

Glasgow Herald

'Bill Knox is a highly skilled professional ... he stamps his books with his own brand of authenticity and accuracy and compelling plotting.'

Irish Times

Printed in Great Britain
by Amazon

39006407R00142